TALENTBORN:AWAKENING

Book 1 of the TalentBorn Series

C. S. Churton

Chapter One

L et me be honest with you: today isn't panning out quite the way I hoped.

Actually, that's putting it mildly. Hell, it's the understatement of the century. If I had to give you a list of ways today could get worse, I'd be drawing a blank. Maybe you're thinking that's because I lack imagination, and maybe you're right, but let me ask you this: how the hell am I, a waitress at the crappiest diner in town, going to get a grand by morning? Because if there's one thing I'm passionate about in this world, it's not getting evicted.

"I'm sorry, Miss Mason, but given your credit rating the bank doesn't feel we're able to offer you a loan at this time," the clerk says, pushing his glasses further up his nose and eyeing me across his immaculate desk.

Translation: We only give money to people who don't need it. I open my mouth to tell the clerk and his condescending smile exactly what I think of that policy. Then I close it again before I make a bad day worse by getting myself thrown out of the bank and publicly humiliated. Besides, it's not his fault I'm having a cash flow problem, even if he is a smug prick. But does he have to sound quite so damned happy about turning me down? It's not like I spent all my money on drugs and alcohol – because that would imply I'd had money to start with.

"Yeah, thanks," I say, snatching up my bag from his desk and stalking from his office before I can follow that with the word 'dickhead'. It's only a short distance from the clerk's office to the bank's front door, but by the time I reach it my self-righteous stalk has been reduced to a defeated shuffle. Shit, what am I going to do? My rent's due tomorrow and I can scrape together maybe half of it. Tips have been way down at the restaurant, and I don't think my landlord will settle for smiles and goodwill.

I let the heavy glass door swing shut behind me as I emerge into the shopping centre, and almost get mowed down by a pair of women pushing buggies with their grubby offspring inside. You know the sort: bottle blonde hair scraped back to show off the type of earrings you hang could your washing on, tank-top at least a size too small, makeup applied with a hand trowel and– Well, I'll spare you the rest. My bag gets knocked right out of my hands, falling to the floor and spilling its contents everywhere. I scowl at the women's oblivious backs, and stoop to grab it. The walking wastes of oxygen don't so much as glance back while I'm picking up my scattered possessions; they're far too busy staring at something shiny in the window of the jewellers.

"Mark said I could choose whichever engagement ring I want," one of them croons in an annoyingly high-pitched voice, jostling her bag-laden buggy as she peers through the window, and paying no attention to the toddler inside it who whines in protest.

"I still can't believe he proposed!"

"I want one with diamonds," Mother-of-the-Year says. "And then matching white gold ones when we get married."

I stop paying attention as I cram the rest of my belongings back into my bag. Bully for them. I'm so glad some people have unlimited money to squander on a ring they're going to wear for a few months. I've seen the price tags on those rings. Any one of them would cover my rent. And don't even get me started on the necklaces. Some of them could pay it for a year. They're right there for the taking.

I seriously did not just think that. I mean, I'm desperate, but I'm not that desperate. The first – and last – thing I ever stole was a chocolate bar. I was nine years old, and I cried all night and took it back the next morning. Anyway, I'm sure places like this have cameras, and– I glance over the prattling pair's shoulders and into the shop. It's busy in there, rammed with weekend shoppers. They probably wouldn't even notice if one of the cheaper rings went missing. Not at first, anyway, and

I'm sure the cameras are focussed on the expensive stuff. I'm not greedy. It hasn't got to be a pricey one. The cheapest item in there would probably do it.

I push open the door almost before I know what I'm doing, letting my long hair fall around my face. You know, in case a camera sees me. I make it four steps inside before my feet stutter to a halt. What in the hell am I doing? I'm a lot of things – not all of them good – but I'm not a thief. I turn around, and for the second time almost get run over by soon-to-be Mrs Waste-of-Oxygen. This time she stops long enough to glare at me like it's my fault she isn't looking where she's going. I smother the childish impulse to flip her off because her toddler's watching me, in between screaming his lungs out.

His doting mother ignores us both and picks up her conversation where it left off.

"I can't wait to show everyone my diamonds!"

"What did Tom say when you broke it off when him?"

"Who says I'm going to? Every girl needs a bit on the side!"

They flounce off towards the most expensive rings in the shop, the loud screech of their cackles trailing in their wake, like nails down a chalkboard.

Stuck up cow. Her, I wouldn't mind stealing from. In what world is it right that someone like that gets showered with expensive gifts while I can barely afford to keep a roof over my head? I'll tell you what world. None. I clench my jaw and pivot on my heel, heading in the opposite direction to the nauseating pair, and let my eyes sweep over the display cabinets. Rings, necklaces and earrings are all perfectly illuminated by subtle backlighting, so that their jewels sparkle and twinkle in their settings. Inside locked cabinets.

There goes that plan. I'm no lock pick, and a smash and grab is going to attract just a little more attention than I'm looking for. It's probably for the best. I'm hardly cut out for a life of crime. I got one of our regulars' orders wrong at the restaurant a few weeks back, and I felt guilty about it for days.

"This way, madam, if you'd like to look in a mirror…"

My head turns to the source of the voice behind me – an impeccably dressed young male sales assistant who's giving his best ingratiating smile to a middle-aged woman with a suspiciously straight nose and a wardrobe that screams designer. I wonder which of them cost her more. She follows him, sweeping her perfect blonde locks aside to admire the gaudy string of pearls hanging around her neck. He doesn't pause to lock the case behind them, leaving it open a crack. I look from the cabinet to the pair and back again. My heart thuds in my chest as I edge

5

closer to it and shoot another glance at the pair. The assistant's attention is firmly on his customer, wearing a smile that looks just the wrong side of genuine, and the woman is lapping up the attention as she flips her hair again. Meanwhile, the display is just sitting there, practically begging a hand to slip inside and relieve it of its extravagant contents. Half a dozen necklaces and matching earrings, and rings that complement the sets. I'm not greedy. I don't need them all. I don't even need a set. Just one ring. That's all I need. All I have to do is take it.

I lift a shaking hand and take another quick look around the room. *Geez, Anna, get it together.* Does anything scream 'guilty' more than a nervous glance over the shoulder? I grit my teeth and ease the door open a crack further, and– Dammit! I'm looking around again before I can stop myself, even while my fingers are fumbling over the nearest ring.

That's when I see them. The two cops talking to a sharply dressed guy who can only be the manager.

If my hand wasn't right inside the display cabinet and my fingers wrapped around the ostentatious ring, I could probably have just walked right out of the store, but it is and they are, and I can barely remember how to breathe, let alone walk. One cop glances in my direction and... I'm not sure if I imagine it, but it looks like he stares at

C. S. CHURTON

me just a moment longer than necessary. Can he see what I'm doing? I'm still staring at him, that's got to be making him suspicious, and dammit, my hand is *still* in the display cabinet. The manager is staring at me, the two cops are staring at me, even some of the customers are turning to look at me, and I'm standing here like a kid with its hand in the cookie jar.

One cop says something to the other and they walk purposefully towards me. Shit. I snap out of my daze and yank my hand from the cabinet, the ring snug against my palm. I turn and make for the door on shaking legs, forcing them to move as fast as they can without breaking into a run. I elbow my way past the Saturday afternoon shoppers, leaving a trail of cross mutters and angry looks in my wake.

"Police, stop!"

I reach the door and break into a run, making right for the crowds in the busiest part of the shopping centre. The whole place is heaving with window shoppers and day trippers, I just need to lose myself in the masses. My feet pound on the tiled floor as I dodge through the thickening crowds, then have to slow to a fast jog – it's too packed to sprint. I leap sideways just in time to keep from ploughing into a mother leading her toddler, and almost bounce straight into a young couple with hands entwined. I duck aside, too breathless to utter an apology, and shut out the angry yells.

What the hell was I thinking? Normal people don't do this. This is not normal behaviour. What a stupid thing to do. I'm so screwed. I should take the ring back and tell them it was a mistake. Tell them I was just looking, or trying it on, or…

But I'm running from cops. Innocent people don't run from cops. It's way too late to play dumb now.

I snatch another look over my shoulder. They're gaining on me. My plan to blend in with the crowd is a bad one because everyone is staring at the idiot running from the cops, and I can't stop running because the cops are right on my heels. And getting closer still.

I collide with someone, a solid thud that knocks the breath from my lungs, and I pivot to see the offending person sprawled on the floor. The old lady's shopping is tossed around her and her walking stick is skidding off to one side. A horrible acidic guilt claws at my throat, but she's not hurt, and if I help her up, I'm caught. I can't get caught. I'll lose everything. My job, my home. I wish I'd thought of all that before dreaming up this stupid, stupid stunt.

I stutter an apology and start tearing through the shoppers again, this time keeping my head firmly forwards. It's easier now. The crowds of shoppers are moving out of my way – which means it's easier for the cops to see me. I need to get out of the shopping centre. I gasp a ragged breath and glance at the shops on either side of me.

There! I spot what I'm looking for up ahead, grit my teeth and push myself harder, ignoring the fire in my chest and ache in my calves. People move aside like the parting of the red sea and I barge through into the discount clothes store, almost bouncing right back off the door in my haste to get through it. My feet scramble for purchase on the tiled floor but somehow don't slide out from under me. I suck in another breath that burns the whole way down and fix my eyes on the escalator on the far side of the store. There's an exit onto the street from the ground floor. If I can get to it, I've got a chance.

I topple a clothing rail behind me, muttering a silent apology to whichever unfortunate is responsible for tidying it up, and push on towards the escalator. I steady myself as I reach it, taking care not to lose my footing. The sound of boots on the metal steps echoes behind me, but I don't dare look at how close my pursuers are. I reach the bottom step and get ready to run again. Something snags my shirt. A hand. I twist and manage to wrench myself free, but as I look across the empty floor to the exit, the second cop appears and cuts me off. I skid to a halt, swivelling my head around frantically. How did he get in front of me? I don't have time to think about it – I have to find a way out. I can't go forward, I can't go back, and I can't let them catch me. I've only got a split second to react, to do something, anything – I've got to get out of here, I've got to–

Chapter Two

I awaken, and for a moment I don't have the first idea where I am. The beige walls blur into focus first, followed by faded furniture and a small TV in need of polishing. I'm in my living room. I twist my head to the right, wincing as the mother of all hangovers makes its presence felt, and see the dust bunnies gathered under the TV stand, which tells me I'm lying on the floor, next to a perfectly good (albeit slightly aged) sofa. The bright light is trying to burn right through my retinas, so I close my eyes and run my mind idly over the crazy dream I'd been having.

Running, a shopping centre, a ring...

The ring! I sit bolt upright, because I remember the ring vividly and I can feel my fingers wrapped around something that's digging into my palm. I slowly force them open, not wanting to look, but my eyes have a will of their own, and they're staring at the white gold band, with tiny diamonds embedded into the elegant design. I blink rapidly, because this ring means it was no dream, and that means that I should be in a cell right now.

I remove the ring from my palm and set it delicately on the floor, squinting at it for a long moment. My head is still foggy and *nothing* about this is making any sort of sense. If it weren't for the tiny midget taking a

11

sledgehammer to my skull from the inside, I'd swear I was still dreaming, but dreams don't normally hurt this much.

I lurch to the kitchen and grab a bottle of water from the fridge, pausing long enough to down half of it and see if the room is going to have the decency to stop spinning, which is apparently overly optimistic. A quick rummage through my junk drawer turns up a box of paracetamol. I wash two of them down with the rest of my water, then stumble back into the living room.

As I settle into the sofa and wait for them to work their magic, I run through the events of yesterday – or was it today? A glance at my phone tells me it's six p.m., and it's still Saturday – I run through the events of this afternoon, but it's a jumbled blur. I remember everything, right up to the bottom of the escalator, when I'd been trapped by the cops. I must've blacked out when I got back here – there's no other reason I'd be sleeping on the floor in the middle of the afternoon – but as for how I got from the scene of my imminent arrest to lying unconscious in my slightly grubby flat? That's a mystery.

With a sigh, I massage my temples and close my eyes. My phone bleeps insistently, and I grope for the silence button to shut off the alarm. Work in one hour. Can I get away with calling in sick? Maybe, but I'd best not chance it. Ed Grant – my less than sympathetic landlord – is threatening to kick me out if I don't stump up the rent by Monday. The ring will cover some of it, most of it if I can sell it for a decent price, but he'll be wanting the rest of the money soon and I can't afford to get fired. Besides, I'm not done freaking out about that damned lump of metal right now, because seriously, what the hell happened back there?

But, much as the thought of passing out, losing three hours and, oh yeah, somehow escaping two cops and then forgetting how I did it terrifies the hell out of me, not being fired is a little more pressing, so I shuffle to the mirror, and attempt to drag a brush through the tangled mess that is my hair. It takes me a full minute to admit that it's a lost cause. I tie it back and focus instead on restoring some colour to my face, courtesy of No7's Stay Perfect range – although at this stage I'd settle for half-way human.

By the time that I admit that, too, is a lost cause and struggle into my waitressing uniform – a mid-length black skirt and white blouse, and flat black shoes that couldn't scream bland any louder if they tried, I've wasted the best part of half an hour. The car broke down a couple of months ago and I haven't had the money to fix it, but even on foot I should just about make it to the restaurant before my shift starts. I snatch up my bag and coat and hurry out of the door, pausing to double lock it behind me, and jog down the two flights of stairs.

Twenty-eight minutes later I swing open the door to The Glasshouse, the place I spend too many hours for not enough pay. Lloyd, the owner-cum-manager and my boss, fancies the place as minimalistic and stylist, but in reality it's sterile, with too much glass and chrome, and not enough atmosphere. We'd been on the brink of closing six months back when Lloyd had struck it lucky and managed to hire the most gifted chef our town has seen in at least a decade. Brendon's too good for this place and is destined for bigger and better things, but for some reason I can't quite fathom, he's decided he likes it here – I know it can't be the pay – and continues to bring in diners from all over town. Lloyd and The Glasshouse will be in a world of trouble when he eventually leaves.

There are already two families and a couple seated at the small tables that aim for intimate but only achieve crowded. The place will be packed when the evening rush starts not long from now. I nod hello to Janey, my fellow waitress and closest friend, then head through to the staff room to dump my stuff.

I pause at the mirror to make another brief attempt at tidying my hair, with no more success than the first time. I force a smile that doesn't reach my eyes and try to put the events of this afternoon out of my mind. It's much easier here, under the restaurant's bright lights, to pretend that it didn't happen, as if it was no more than a disturbing dream to be chased away by the morning sun.

"Jesus, Anna, you look like hell."

Or not. Tact is not Janey's strong point. I meet her eyes in the mirror and smile sadly, unable to fall into our usual easy banter. Janey's smile falters.

"What's wrong?" she asks, pulling me around for a gentle embrace. I collapse into her and feel tears forming in my eyes, threatening to ruin my already-awful makeup. Janey steers me to a chair and I sit, biting my lip. I don't even know where to start – or how much I can tell her. I want to tell her everything and have her tell me that it's okay, but I know that it's not and I can't bear the thought of her knowing I'm a thief. I take a shaky breath and will the tears back into my eyes before they can do any damage.

"This morning I was..." Was what? Stealing a five-hundred-pound ring from a jewellers? Running from the police? About to be arrested? "... in town, in the shopping centre, and I... I think I blacked out. I woke up at home, but I don't know how I got there. Something's... something's wrong with me, I know it, I–"

I stop and suck in a juddering breath, and she grabs the seat opposite me and takes my hand in hers.

"Look at me, Anna. It's going to be okay. We'll get to the bottom of this." She catches a stray lock of my hair and tucks it behind my ear. "And you're going to see a doctor, okay?"

She arches a brow with a stern look on her face, and I nod meekly. She knows how I feel about doctors. Well, needles, anyway, and our local doc takes any opportunity to stick you. But she's right. I need to get checked out and find out what caused it, even if it's a one-off. And it had better be a one-off.

"Did someone take you home? Maybe you passed out and someone took you back."

"No, I don't think so. I locked up before I left, and I woke up inside."

"Hm, you must have passed out after you got back home then," she muses. "But if you don't remember it– Did you hit your head?"

"I don't think so, but I've got the worst headache."

"Are you sure you're okay to be here? Because I can handle this shift without you."

I nod quickly. I need the money, and I need the distraction. Janey searches my face for a long moment, and then nods.

"Right then, we'd best get out there before Lloyd has our hides."

She squeezes my hand and gets up, and I follow her out of the room, my smile a little less forced than it had been a few minutes ago.

*

I made it through the rest of the shift without having a breakdown – no small miracle – largely thanks to my decision to pretend the whole thing never happened. I'm still a little shaken about it all when I get up the next morning, but whatever. The whole thing was probably down to stress. I put myself in a stupid situation; it's no wonder my brain decided to shut down and take a little time out. I can't explain how I got away from the police, but maybe I got lucky, caught them off guard and pushed past or something.

Anyway, it doesn't matter. I'm feeling much better this morning, and I'm going to speak to a guy I know about the ring, so with any luck it'll be gone by this afternoon. I'll still be short on the rent, even with my tips from the restaurant last night, but as long as I give Ed something I'm sure he'll let it slide. Probably.

Honestly, I can't get rid of the damned thing soon enough. Incriminating evidence aside, I don't need any reminders of my moment of insanity staring me in the face. There's no time like the present, especially when it comes to ridding yourself of stolen property.

I grab my phone and search through for Mike's number. If you're busy judging me for not only knowing someone who can offload a stolen ring, but also having his number saved in my phone, then calm down. It was after I met him that I found out about his casual disregard for the law. I already told you: I don't normally go in for this sort of thing. Anyway, we all know someone a bit dodgy, right? The phone rings for a while before voicemail cuts in, but even I'm not dumb enough to leave a message.

I'll send a text instead. I type and delete the message several times, gnawing on my nails; after all, I don't want to leave behind anything to incriminate myself – aside from the half dozen witnesses at the shopping centre yesterday, that is. I trust Mike, but he's a bit of a ladies' man and I don't want to risk anyone else picking up the message. Best to keep it vague, and just ask him to phone me. I tap out the message and hit send, then put my phone in my pocket so I'll hear it when he calls back.

I'm at a bit of a loose end until he does, so I grab the vacuum from its hiding place and tackle the dust bunnies lurking under the sofa. If nothing else, waking up on the floor made me realise that I really need to get on top of the cleaning in here. I'm not a slob or anything, but I'd be lying if I said that I hadn't let my standards slip with the stress of trying to get enough shifts at the restaurant.

I crank up the radio and sing along with Dolly complaining about the injustices of working nine to five (the chance would be a fine thing) as I move around the flat. The drone of the hoover drowns out my tuneless singing, a blessing which is surpassed only by the fact that there is no-one to see me dancing around the room with the vacuum pipe in hand.

There's a knock at the door, which I can just make out above the noise. I turn off the vacuum and reach over to kill Dolly. A quick glance confirms the security chain is on before I open the door the couple of inches it allows. We don't get too much trouble around here, but it pays to be cautious – I'm not expecting anyone. Maybe Janey's stopped by and make sure I've booked an appointment with the doctor (I haven't), or maybe Ed's come to see if he can get his rent early. I wish I'd thought of that before I started to open the door, but it's too late to pretend I'm not home now.

The face I see through the gap doesn't belong to Ed or Janey. In fact, I don't recognise it at all. It's a man, maybe late twenties or early thirties, with short dark hair, blue eyes, and clean shaven. He's above averagely good looking, and I'd be showing him my best smile if he wasn't wearing a suit. Suits make me suspicious.

"Yes?"

"Anna Mason?" he asks, reaching into his pocket and producing an ID card with his face on it. Shit, he's a cop. I definitely shouldn't have opened the door. How did he find me? I consider slamming the door in his face, but that would be almost as stupid as what I did yesterday. There's no other way out of the flat – I'm on the second floor, so the window's hardly an option. Plus, where would I run? This is my home. He knows where I live. He knows who I am.

"I'll take that as a yes. My name's Scott Logan. Can I come in?"

I start to shake my head, and then stop myself. I need to make him think he's got me mixed up with someone else. He's not one of the cops from yesterday, so he can't be certain it was me. I just have to act innocent.

"Okay, one second."

I close the door briefly and remove the chain. I take a deep breath and try to compose myself as I open it again. And then I remember: the ring! It's sitting on the table, waiting for Mike to call me back. There's no way the cop can miss it, and I can hardly claim mistaken identity when I've been caught red-handed. The door swings open and he steps across the threshold. I glance backwards over my shoulder at the ring and then curse myself – do I never learn? I need to get hold of it before he sees it; I need to get it out of here. *I* need to get out of here. Grab the ring, or push past him out of the door? My heart's in my throat and all I know is I need to do something before it's too late, I've got to–

Chapter Three

I come to with a jolt. The first thing I'm aware of is a buzzing against my hip. My phone. I ignore it. I'm lying on my side and the pounding in my head is back. I groan and roll over, then freeze as a cold dampness spreads along my back. Great. Just great.

Out of respect for my splitting headache, I open my eyes slowly. I have got to stop getting carried away with Janey's crazy drinking games. That girl is a bad influence. Except… I look around as much as I can without moving my head. I'm lying in a dirty puddle, with a patch of grey sky above me. A cold unease wells in my stomach. This is a little much for a girls' night out… and, now that I think about it, I don't remember getting ready to go out. Where the hell am I?

I sit up slowly, then screw my eyes shut as the pain intensifies tenfold. I shuffle back to a wall and lean against it, resting my head against the damp brickwork. While I'm sitting there, on the dirty, wet floor with no regard for the perfectly good pair of jeans I'm ruining, I try to remember how I got here.

I wasn't with Janey. I was in my flat, I remember that much. And I remember that guy – Scott – coming to the door, and I remember that damned ring sitting on the table, but then – nothing. It's like I blacked out there and woke up here. Except that's not possible, because there's no way I walked down two flights of stairs and to wherever the hell I am whilst unconscious. Literally no way. I've never sleep-walked, and I'm pretty sure to sleep-walk you need to actually be asleep rather than unconscious. Maybe Scott brought me here. Yeah, right. If I blacked out in front of him, he'd have had to call an ambulance. Cops aren't allowed to just leave you lying there, and they're certainly not allowed to dump you in an alley filled with questionable smells. Assuming he was really a cop.

I force myself to take a breath and think. He had an ID card, but I wasn't close enough to see it properly. How was it he introduced himself? Scott Logan, not PC or DC Scott Logan. And I'm sure I remember reading somewhere they have to identify themselves as police officers, otherwise their actions aren't legal. Or maybe I made that up, I don't know. All I know is that something isn't right.

The pounding has eased up, so I open my eyes again and look around me. I have no idea where I am. It looks like an alleyway between two blocks of flats. There's a pile of rubbish sacks piled up at the bottom of some rusted metal stairs leading to a fire exit, some of them split open and spewing their rotting contents onto the floor. I can see people walking past the alleyway, going about their business – fortunately none of them are looking my way because I'd have a hard job explaining what I'm doing here. I push myself to my feet and try to brush down my jeans, but that's a lost cause. All I'm doing is smearing the dirt even further and making my hands filthy.

I step out into the street, ignoring the looks my grubby clothing gets. I don't recognise the street, but Whitelyn is a pretty big town, and I've only lived here a few years, so that's not really a surprise. I pull up the maps feature on my phone, and blink at the pulsing dot.

I'm not in Whitelyn anymore. I'm twenty miles away.

This is crazy.

A wheezing sound rattles around my ears, and it takes me a moment to realise it's my breathing, coming in ragged gasps. I take a step back into the alleyway and collapse against the wall. I'm twenty miles away from home. How am I twenty miles away from home? I was in my flat, I was right there in my flat! I can't be out here miles away. I lift the phone in my shaking hand and stare at the map, but the dot hasn't moved. And the clock at the top says I only passed out half an hour ago. The phone slips through my fingers and clatters to the damp floor. There's no way I sleep-walked twenty miles in half an hour, not to mention all the roads I'd have to have crossed without being noticed, or hit by a car... It's just not possible. Literally not possible. *None* of this is possible. I slide to the floor beside my phone as the prickly heat builds up behind my eyes. Within seconds, the sobs are racking my body and burning my throat, and I lower my head onto my arms and give in to them. My life is spiralling out of control; there's something wrong with me, something seriously wrong, and I'm so scared, more scared even than I had been in the jewellers when the police saw me stealing that stupid ring.

My eyes are burning and there's an awful sound coming out of me but I can't stop it, don't even want to stop it. If I listen to the sound I don't have to think about the blackouts, the police, the fact that I'm sitting in a dirty alley, miles from home – a home that I won't have come next week because there's no way I can get the rest of the rent money in time.

Something lands on my shoulder, and I jump with a loud gasp. There's a guy staring down at me.

"I'm sorry," he says, removing his hand and stepping back. "I didn't mean to startle you. I was just walking past, and I heard you..." He indicates the street and trails off as he looks at me. "Are you okay?"

I start to nod but I don't have the energy to lie. I give up and shake my head. I'm not okay. Not even close. My Good Samaritan looks uneasy for a moment, but then smiles and crouches down beside me. I watch him closely as he picks up my phone and holds it out to me.

"Here, I think you dropped this."

I stretch out my hand and take it from him, and stare at the blank screen. It's on standby mode, but I can still see that horrifying image in my mind.

"My name's Nathan, what's yours, love?"

"Anna," I manage after a moment.

"Come on, let's get you up," he suggests, rising to his feet and offering me his hand. I eyeball his outstretched limb for a moment before letting him take my hand and pull me to my feet.

"You're soaked," he says. "Have you been out here long?"

I don't answer, and he starts talking again. I stare at his lips and try to make myself focus on his words.

"Do you want to go to the hospital?" he's asking.

"No," I answer in a whisper, not sure if he can hear me. "I just want to go home."

"Where do you live?" he asks. I tell him and he frowns. "You're a long way from home – what are you doing here?"

That's the million-dollar question, but if I try to explain he's definitely going to want to take me to the hospital, and I'm cold and tired and I just want to sleep. And maybe see if I have any more paracetamol to shift this headache. I take the easy option and shrug.

"Okay, well, my car's just around the corner. Come on, I'll give you a lift."

I don't know how long it takes us to get back to my flat. Most of the journey passes in a blur, and although I'm sure Nathan tried to make conversation along the way, I can't remember a word he said. All I keep thinking is that there's no physical way I could have walked twenty miles without knowing it. Or run, or whatever.

"Well, here we are," he says, as he stops the car outside my block and looks across at me.

"Thank you," I say in a monotone.

"Look, are you sure you don't... are you going to be okay?"

"I'll be fine," I say, clicking open the door and stepping out. "Thanks."

I can feel his eyes on me as I shut the door and walk into my block. I put him out of my mind. I have bigger things to worry about, like my visitor from earlier and that stupid ring. At least I can do something about one of them. Everything else can wait. Forever, preferably.

I get my phone out as I let myself into my flat and key in a number. A familiar voice answers on the third ring.

"Hello?"

"Mike, hi. It's Anna. I've got something here; a ring. Are you interested?"

"Yeah, I might be," he says. "Although I was hoping it was me you wanted, not my money."

I can hear the smile in his voice, and my lips twitch as I flop down onto the sofa. Mike never misses an opportunity to flirt. He's not such a bad guy either. And if he wasn't more prone to straying than a feral cat, I'd probably be tempted. But I'm willing to bet it's not much fun waiting to see what he drags in each night.

"Sorry, Mike, strictly business."

"C'mon, girl, you're breaking my heart," he says, and then he gets serious. "Alright, tell me about this ring."

"It's white gold, with diamonds. Classy," I assure him, turning it over in my hands.

"And where did you get it?"

"Do you really care?" I ask.

"I guess not," he says. "Just… It's not an engagement ring, is it? I don't want you to go changing your mind on me."

"Don't worry, that's not going to happen." I definitely don't want to see this ring again. It's caused me more than enough trouble for one lifetime.

"Alright. Can you come by my place this evening?"

"You aren't going to try to woo me, right? Because you know I'm immune to your so called 'charms'."

He laughs, and I can hear his smile when he promises,

"Strictly business. Unless you change your mind."

With a smile of my own, I cut the connection and put the phone down with a sigh. I'll soon be shot of this damned ring, and hopefully all the trouble it's brought me. I reach for my laptop and fire it up, drumming my fingers on the arm of the chair as it reluctantly comes to life. I know I should really see a doctor, but it's not like anyone will see me on a Sunday afternoon, and besides, I've got to see Mike, so Doctor Google will have to do for now.

I pull up the site and type in 'medical, blackouts, losing time'. I scroll through the first half dozen websites that come up, and by the time I'm done I've diagnosed myself with everything from panic attacks to a brain tumour. Maybe this wasn't such a great idea.

And what if it isn't medical at all? What if it's something else… something unthinkable? The first time I blacked out I was running from the cops, the second time was when the suit came to the door. Maybe it's something to do with them. Maybe it's something to do with him. Maybe it's something to do with this damned ring. I don't know. I bite back a scream of frustration. I just want some answers. Is that really so much to ask?

I stop and think for a minute, then delete my search and slowly type in 'police weapons, blackouts'. I know it doesn't make any sense. I know that the police in this country don't carry weapons – but then what about this does make sense? As I read through the first-hand accounts of people who have been tasered and sprayed with PAVA, I start wondering if there's more to this than I first thought. Maybe the guy in the suit did do something. I mean, why wasn't he waiting here for me when I got back? Not that I'm ungrateful to still have my freedom, but I was caught red-handed. He had me cornered, and he had the ring, and he, what, just walked away without either? Seems like a stretch.

Maybe it's something in the ring that's causing my blackouts. None of this started until after I first touched it. But I quickly rule that out, firstly because it's the most ridiculous thing I've come up with so far, and secondly because I wasn't even touching it when I blacked out the last time.

I sigh and lean back in my chair. Conspiracy theories are one thing, but this is getting ridiculous. I switch off the computer before I can drive myself completely mad, and pace around the flat. I pass the fridge and realise I haven't eaten since yesterday afternoon. Maybe that explains my sudden onset of insanity. I'm not one of these girls who can skip meals without serious consequences. Usually it's just crankiness, though. I pull open the fridge door and have a rummage, but it's a lost cause.

I'll get some food at the restaurant. Lloyd will let me scrounge a free meal, and the walk will do me good.

I'm a bit calmer when I get to The Glasshouse. It's pretty much deserted – Brendon's shift doesn't start until this evening, and most of our regulars know his work schedule. I nod to Lucy, the new girl Lloyd's taken on to work Sundays, and claim a quiet seat in the corner.

I pick up the menu and stare at it blankly, wondering if the day chef is can actually cook any of this. Brendon redesigned the entire menu when Lloyd took him on, and I'm not sure some fresh out of catering school kid can pull off any of his creations. On the other hand, it's pretty much guaranteed to be better than anything I could concoct from the meagre contents of my fridge.

I hear the chair opposite me creak, and I lower my menu to treat my unwanted companion to my fiercest frown.

"This table's..." I stop mid-sentence as I catch sight of the man sitting across the table. It's the suit from this morning – Scott Logan – smiling benignly as though he hasn't come to tear my life apart. I stand abruptly, casting a glance at the exit, sending my chair tumbling onto its side.

"Whoa, take it easy," he says, raising his hands.

"Take it easy?" I demand, stunned by his gall. But he hasn't made any move to stop me leaving, which is...

unexpected. Like anything about this week is panning out the way I expected.

"I just want to talk to you," he says, lowering his hands onto the table, and keeping them there, palms down. "Why don't you sit down?"

He nods at my toppled chair. I hesitate. On the one hand, I need some answers. On the other, bad things happen when this guy shows up. Keeping my eyes firmly fixed on him, I right the chair, but don't sit on it. He raises an eyebrow, apparently amused by my caution.

"Last time you showed up, I blacked out. I don't feel like sitting."

"You..." His forehead wrinkles above concerned blue eyes. Either he's genuinely confused or he's one hell of an actor. Or a sociopath. Let's not rule that out. "Wait, you don't know what you're doing?"

"What *I'm* doing?" I hiss. "I want to know what *you* did to me, you bastard. I woke–" I glance around and lower my voice. "I woke up with a pounding headache, lying in an alleyway God knows where."

"I didn't do that." He seems sincere, but again, so do sociopaths.

"No? Then who did?"

"You."

I stare at him, searching his eyes and trying to work out what he's getting at.

"You mean I'm... passing out."

"You're doing a little more than that." He gestures at the chair. "Please, sit."

Slowly, I pull out the chair and perch on the edge. I've never noticed how uncomfortable The Glasshouse's chairs are before. If I want to hear what he's got to say – and I think I do – then I need to play along. His hands are back on the table; if he reaches for a weapon, a taser or whatever, then I should have plenty of warning. In theory.

"I'm sitting. Now tell me what's going on."

"You really don't know?"

"Know what?" I demand, my hands clenching into fists. I take a moment to force the tension from them.

"That you're shifting."

"Shifting?"

"Or phasing, teleporting, whatever you want to call it. So far as I can tell."

I pause, waiting for the punchline. He's serious.

"You're crazy." I can feel myself shaking as I get to my feet, my chair scraping loudly across the floor.

"Anna, calm down. Just hear me out."

"You're crazy," I repeat. "Stay away from me."

I back away, and then turn for the exit. Walking towards me is the Good Samaritan from this morning. He nods a greeting to the suit behind me. I gasp. How does he... how do they–? What do they want with me? I've got to get out of here. I've got to get away from them. I've got to–

Chapter Four

I know I'm alive because being dead can't possibly hurt this much. My head is literally exploding. Well, okay, probably not literally, but I'd have to move to check that, and I'm pretty sure that's not an option right now. I lie still, eyes closed, and take a mental inventory. Arms and legs feel okay, fingers and toes wiggle. Head feels like it's split in half. I'm on my back, and it's damp. I rub my fingers along the floor. Grass. I'm lying on damp grass.

I force my eyes open to stare up at the grey expanse above me and immediately start to gag. I roll onto my side and retch a couple of times, but my stomach has nothing to cough up. Small mercies and all that. I roll back flat and close my eyes again, focussing on the sensation of air entering and leaving my lungs. I tried meditation once, years ago, but I never had the patience. All that 'feel the air moving through your body, breathe your connection to the earth' stuff wasn't up my street. It doesn't seem so bad now, though. After a minute or two of just breathing, the pain in my head subsides to the point I can think.

These blackouts are coming way too frequently for my comfort. What was it Scott had called it? Shifting? But shifting what? Shifting where? From the restaurant to here – wherever here is? I groan, but this time not from pain. I've got even more questions than before I spoke to him. Like my Good Samaritan from this morning. They obviously know each other, but I'm not sure what that means. I am sure it can't be a good thing, though. Like maybe he's following me or something. And now I sound crazy *and* paranoid. Great.

I forget about the second guy for the moment. He's making my head hurt worse than it already was, and I've got enough on my plate without worrying about him.

I sit up slowly and open my eyes. At least this time I don't have the urge to vomit. I know this place. It's a playing field about two miles from my flat. Usually it's filled with kids kicking footballs about, and dog walkers yelling at their unruly charges, but luckily for me it's deserted, probably thanks to the foul weather. I'm not up to dealing with any more knights in shining armour, planted or otherwise.

I try to put what Scott said from my mind. He's obviously a few pennies short of a pound. Except... well, much as I hate to admit it, it makes more sense than anything I've come up with. The medical stuff on Google could account for the blackouts and the memory loss, but it couldn't even come close to explaining how I managed to escape two cops who had me cornered, and get out of my flat when Scott was standing between me and the only exit. At least his theory could explain that.

I can't believe I'm actually considering this nonsense. Maybe I hit my head when I blacked out. Either way, the middle of a damp field probably isn't the best place to think things through.

I push myself up off the damp ground for the second time today and check my phone. Two thirty. I've been out for nearly two hours. I shuffle out of the park through the painted green metal gate and start heading towards home. Not that it's going to be home for much longer if I can't convince Mike to buy the ring for a decent amount. My impending arrest and possible descent into insanity haven't changed the fact that I still have the same problems I had yesterday morning. If I can't raise the rent money, I'll be out on the streets come tomorrow night.

I pause. Has it seriously only been a day since all of this started? I run back through everything that's happened and conclude that, yes, it really has been less than twenty-four hours since I stole the ring. And I've spent a large amount of that time unconscious.

I thrust my hands into my pockets and carry on shuffling along the street. It's in one of the nicer parts of town – the wide pavements are clean and well maintained, and lined with spacious two-up, two-down houses, each with a small but immaculate front garden, two cars and a garage.

It's hard to miss the sliding scale of disrepair as I keep moving. The gravelled driveways and freshly painted facades are replaced by crumbling paving stones and aged brickwork. By the time I'm home, the only trace of paint is the illegible graffiti, the street lamps are few and far between, and the air is heavy with a pungent mix of fox urine and rotting waste.

I open the door to my block and trudge up the two flights of concrete steps. I pause outside my front door and rummage through my bag for the key, whilst making a mental note to either remove some of the junk from it or buy a bigger bag. But I like this bag. It goes with, like, ninety percent of my wardrobe. And I need all the stuff I've got inside it. I mean, I'm not sure exactly what's in its depths, but I'm sure I put it all there for a reason.

I finally get through the door, and close it with my foot as I drop the key back in my bag. I look up and yelp, the bag falling from my grasp. There's a man standing in the corner. I open my mouth to scream, and then recognise him as the suit. Scott. I watch him as I fumble for the door handle behind my back. I haven't ruled out screaming yet, either.

"Don't be afraid," he says, raising his hands like he's trying to calm a wild animal.

"Don't be afraid?" I snap, my voice shaking almost as much as my hands. "You've broken into my home! How do you expect me to feel?"

"I'm not here to hurt you," he promises in his all-too-sincere voice. "I'm not carrying a weapon."

He eases off his suit jacket, holds it out to the side and lets it drop on the floor, then untucks his shirt and turns slowly in a circle so I can see he's telling the truth. Which means nothing, because we both know he could overpower me if he wanted. He sees I'm not impressed and nods, his expression thoughtful.

"I'm going to sit down, okay?"

I purse my lips but release my grip on the door handle. Scott attempts to lower himself to the floor while keeping his hands raised. If I wasn't so scared I'd laugh, but I am, and I don't.

"I know," he says, flashing me a boyish smile. "About as graceful as a three-legged elephant with an inner ear infection. And getting back up isn't going to be any prettier." The smile fades and his eyes hold mine.

"I just want to talk to you Anna, I promise. Tell me what I need to do to show you I'm on your side."

"Not breaking into my home would be a good start."

"Okay, well, if it helps, I didn't break in. I picked the lock."

I shake my head in disbelief.

"No, that doesn't help. How would that help?"

My voice is bordering on hysterical. I turn away and take a deep breath, and then realise I have my back to him. I spin back around and see his eyes sparkle with amusement.

"Just tell me what you want and leave, before I call the cops."

"You might want to get rid of that ring before you call the boys in blue," he says, nodding his head at the cause of all my troubles, still sitting on the table where I'd left it.

"So I was right, then. You're not a cop."

He stares at me for a moment, and I stare back, trying to decipher his expression. I've never been much good at reading people, although I wish I was – half of me wants to hear him out, and the other half is screaming at me to run full pelt into the nearest police station. I'm pretty sure that whatever the sentence is for stealing a ring, this guy is capable of far worse.

"That was smart," he acknowledges with a note of respect in his voice. "You're right, I'm not. I work for... well, we'll get to that."

He lowers his hands, apparently content that I'm done freaking out. I'm not so sure. I glance at the door, double checking I haven't put the security chain on, in case I need to leave in a hurry.

"We've got a lot to talk about," he says softly. "Why don't you sit? I'll stay right here."

It seems like every time I see this guy he's asking me to sit down. I'm starting to get an idea how it feels to be a dog. But my legs are feeling weak, and if I'm not going to run, sitting is probably a good idea. I take a tentative step to the sofa – the seat that's closest to the door – and perch on the edge.

"I'm listening." My voice is a hoarse whisper that I barely recognise.

"Let me ask you something," he says. "Do you really believe you're just blacking out?"

"Yes." *No.* I'm torn between thinking he's the one doing this to me, and believing what he said in the restaurant. But his theories are so crazy, I don't want to say them out loud. Apparently, though, he has no such reservations.

"I'm not a hundred percent sure what you're doing, but twice today you've disappeared right in front of my eyes."

"That's..." I grope for the right word and realise there isn't one. "You're insane."

"As insane as blacking out in your flat and waking up in an alleyway? What do you think, that you're sleep-walking? Suffering from amnesia?"

My cheeks colour. Somehow he's made my leading theory sound more ridiculous than vanishing into thin air.

"The first time you blacked out – that we know of – you managed to get away from two police officers who were right on top of you. If you'd just passed out, don't you think you'd have woken up in a cell?"

"That was the first time," I confirm quietly, not wanting to address his other question. Because he's right, of course. It was one of the first things I thought of when I came around, and what I've been trying not to think about ever since.

He nods and exhales slowly.

"Yeah, I thought that might be why you were so spooked. Okay, look, it's not my job to convince you that you're doing this. You'll figure that out for yourself soon enough."

"What is your job?" I ask, because if he's not a cop, and not a sociopath – although let's not be too hasty in writing that one off – I'd like to know what the hell he is.

"I work for the government, for the Abnormal Genetics Research Department. AbGen."

He's watching me carefully in case I freak out. And I won't lie, the only reason I haven't run away screaming is because my legs have turned to jelly. The government? When has that ever been a good thing? And "Research Department"? Those words alone conjure some pretty terrifying images of being chained up in some underground lab out in the country. I must have glanced at the door again, because he says,

"Don't run out on me just yet. I can help you. You're having some pretty bad side effects right now. What if we can help you stop the black outs?"

"You can stop them?" The words pop out of my mouth before I can decide if I want to ask them. Scott raises one hand in a steadying gesture.

"I don't want to make any promises I can't keep. We *might* be able to help you stop them. But don't you think it's worth finding out? My colleague tells me you were in a pretty bad state this morning."

He's right, again. It's only been a day, but already there's not much I wouldn't do to stop these black outs, or whatever they are.

"What do I have to do?"

"Come in with me," he says. "Have a chat with our guys. Any time you want to leave, you can."

"Any time?" I say, not that I'm really considering it. I'd have to be crazy to consider it.

"Any time," he agrees with a nod. "And it's not like we could stop you, if you did your shifting thing, right?"

I glance at the clock on the wall, and remember my meet with Mike. I want to get to the bottom of these black outs, but I also very much want not to get evicted.

43

"I can't. I have to meet a guy and get some money to pay the rent." I play the words back in my head and hope they didn't sound as bad as I think they did. Scott at least didn't seem to notice. Instead, he moves his hand slowly to his pocket, and pulls something out. He holds it up so I can see it's a phone.

"Don't panic on me, okay?" he says with a smile, and then dials a number. He waits for someone to answer – I wonder if it's the Good Samaritan – and then speaks curtly.

"Yeah, go ahead and transfer the money."

He waits another moment and then cuts the connection, and places the phone on the floor where I can see it.

"It's done."

"What's done?"

"Your rent's paid up for the next three months."

"You've... paid my landlord?"

"You can call him and check if you want," Scott offers. I shake my head mutely. After a moment, I gather my wits.

"And all I have to do is go with you?" I ask.

He shakes his head.

"No, Anna, this isn't a bribe. The money's yours, whatever you decide to do, but I hope you'll come with

44

me. I want to help you. I know you don't think it right now, but we are the good guys."

"Why would you do that?" I manage, still stunned by his actions, by the ease with which he had wiped out months of debt.

"Call it a gesture of good faith." His phone beeps: a text message. He picks it up and glances at the screen, his face unchanging, and then looks at me again.

"And here's another one. The police have just pulled up outside. I can get you past them, but you're out of time. You need to decide: are you coming, or staying?"

I hesitate for less than half a second.

"Coming." It's not the cops, or the money. I need answers, and so far, Scott is the only one who seems to have any idea what's going on. Even if it does sound crazy.

He nods and rises to his feet.

"Let's go, then." He stoops to collect his jacket and pulls it on, then takes my arm. I tense at the contact, and he smiles apologetically.

"We'd best make this look real."

He opens the door and I allow him to steer me through it, just as two cops crest the stairs. They stop and look at us. At me, to be precise. I recognise one as the cop who chased me yesterday morning. The other I haven't seen before.

"PCs Drake and Russell," the cop from yesterday identifies himself and his partner, holding out his warrant card. "Stay where you are."

"Take it easy, boys," Scott says, withdrawing his own ID card. "DS Yates, from Ryebridge station."

"You're a little outside of your patch," the second cop says, eyeing him coldly.

"That's 'You're a little outside of your patch, *Sarge*'," Scott corrects him. The cop's jaw clenches. "And that would be because we've had her under surveillance for the last week."

"Then why weren't we told?"

"It's need to know, and I guess you didn't. Now, if you don't mind?"

The two cops reluctantly part, and Scott steers me through the gap. I walk beside him unresisting as we start to descend the stairs, processing everything he's said.

"You swore you weren't a cop," I hiss.

"Relax," he says, casting a glance over his shoulder to make sure we're out of earshot. "It's a fake."

Nothing about that sentence particularly makes me want to relax, but at this stage I'm committed. There's no going back – literally – so I let him escort me outside. The door has barely shut behind us when a car pulls up at the curb, coming to a halt behind the marked police car.

"He's with us," Scott says. I recognise both the vehicle and its driver from this morning at the alleyway. The man is heavily built, all of it muscle. He's wearing the same faded brown jacket he had on this morning, with the collar turned up, and under it a shirt and tie. I guess this 'AbGen' group don't go for casual wear.

Scott opens one of the rear doors and I slide inside. The door slams shut behind and I put my seatbelt on. Scott walks round and gets into the passenger seat. He casts a glance at me over his shoulder.

"I gather you two have already met."

The driver twists round and gives me a friendly smile. There's a small scar to one side of his brown eyes, and his nose has a bulge in the middle where it's clearly been broken at least once. I get why they send Scott to meet people first. Even with the smile, it's obvious this guy is no stranger to trouble.

"Nathan Webb," he reminds me. "I hope you're feeling better."

I give him a tight smile in return. I'm feeling a lot of things right now, but I'm pretty sure none of them are 'better'. The main one is vulnerable. Nathan saw me on the verge of a break down this morning. The only person who's seen me cry before is Janey, and we go back a long way. I would never normally drop my guard in front of someone I don't know. And if it's uncomfortably intimate for a stranger to see you cry, trust me when I say it's even more uncomfortable to see that person again, and sit in a confined space with them making awkward conversation.

The engine turns over and the car pulls away, and it doesn't matter anymore. I'm trapped back here; I've got no choice other than to go with them, short of jumping out of a moving car. And I'm pretty sure in real life that doesn't end well. Of course, Scott says I can leave whenever I want, but if he changes his mind, there's not much I can do about it. He meets my eye in the rear-view mirror, then turns to look at me. He has that calming-a-wild-animal look again.

"You okay back there?"

I nod, although I'm not. I haven't been okay since this whole thing started. Who could possibly be okay with this? But one of them has already seen me cry, the other made me scream; I don't want to seem like any more of a coward than I already do.

"Stop the car," he says quietly. Nathan looks at him, then signals and pulls the car over to the side of the road. He switches off the engine.

"I don't want you to be afraid, Anna," Scott tells me. "For one thing, if you get too scared, you're going to shift again, and for another, I think you've spent enough of the last twenty-four hours afraid, am I right?"

I stare back at him mutely.

"I meant what I said," he promises. "Any time you want to leave, I won't stop you. If you want to get out of the car right now, it's up to you."

I'd be crazy not to – I'm sitting in a car with two guys I met for the first time this morning, who've already admitted to working for a shady government organisation and impersonating police officers, and I have no clue where they're taking me. Not to mention that they keep talking about me 'shifting' as if it's a perfectly normal thing.

"I want to keep going."

I guess crazy is the order of the day. Scott nods, and the car starts up again and eases out into the traffic. Nathan turns a dial and warm air starts to pump into the vehicle. I realise that I'm shivering, but I doubt it's from the cold. But I have to find out how to stop these black outs, and I can't deny that I'm curious about who Scott works for. This 'AbGen' group doesn't seem bothered about playing by the rules. What do they get up to when they're not tracking down waitresses?

I have about a hundred questions but I can't figure out how to word any of them, so instead I settle back into my seat. We ride in silence for maybe half an hour, the scenery changing from houses and street lights to trees and fields lining motorways. It doesn't take long to lose track of where we're going, but if I really wanted, I could

49

use the maps feature on my phone to find out where we are. I don't. I've decided to trust Scott. I chose to stay in the car, so there's no point in trying to guess where we're headed. I'll know soon enough anyway.

Nathan is a conscientious driver – he's fast but careful, moving into the outer lanes to pass other drivers and then dropping back inside again. He checks his mirrors constantly, and so does Scott, and I wonder if they're checking to see if we're being followed, or if it's just habit. Hopefully the latter.

He signals onto a slip road and leaves the motorway. We must be getting close. My stomach starts to churn. Maybe I should have just gone and seen the doctor tomorrow, and he could have diagnosed me with something nice and normal, or said I was under too much stress. The last thing I need is to be going into some secret government facility to meet some people who may or may not want to poke around inside my brain.

"Take a deep breath, Anna," Scott says, and I look up from my feet to see him watching me. I realise I can hear rapid breathing – my own – and make an effort to slow it down. It's not happening.

"You're going to be fine." He keeps saying that, but how do I know I can trust him, really? I know nothing about him other than his name, which may or may not be real. After all, he carries a fake police ID card, so it's not like it bothers him to lie about who he is. My mother never gave me much advice, but not getting into cars with strangers was at the top of the list. Of course, she also told me never to stay in the same place for too long, so maybe paranoia runs in the family.

"Do you want me to stop the car?"

It comes back to the same thing. Because every time he asks me that, it reminds me I've got nothing to go back to. This is the only way I can find out what's going on and get back some sort of control over my life. I shake my head in response and make another attempt to control my breathing. I focus on each breath as it enters my lungs, lingers a while and then leaves again, until my breathing is slow and steady. I always knew those meditation classes would come in handy one day. Deep down. Somewhere. Mrs Steadman would have been proud.

I spend the rest of the journey listening to my breathing and trying not to think too much about where we're going and what might happen when we get there. I don't know how much longer it is before the car comes to a stop. Scott turns in his seat to look at me.

"Are you ready?"

Chapter Five

I don't think it's necessarily a good idea to answer that question honestly, so I just nod and thrust my hands into my pockets where he can't see them shaking. If nothing else, I'll be glad for the waiting to be over. They get out of the car and I do the same, looking around me. We're on what looks like a normal road – there are several blocks of offices and a couple of shops. Beyond them, I can see houses. It's not what I was expecting, but I'm way past being surprised by now.

I follow Scott up several steps to an oak door with a speaker beside it. He pauses and meets my eye.

"What you're about to see, you can't tell anyone."

"Or you'll have to kill me?"

"I'm serious, Anna. This organisation doesn't officially exist; *we* don't exist. And neither will you if you choose to join us."

The smile drops from my face and I nod. *Bloody hell, Anna, what are you getting yourself into?* Scott searches my eyes for a moment longer and seems content that I get it. His attention turns to the speaker, and he presses the buzzer beside it. Almost immediately a voice asks him to identify himself.

"Agents Logan and Webb. We have a guest."

"Is the street secure?" the monotone voice asks.

"There's a party across the road," Scott answers. I look over my shoulder but don't see any sign of the party.

"It's a code," he explains, catching my glance. "If I say the street's clear they'll know I've been compromised."

I want to ask what happens if he's been compromised, but before I get the chance there is a buzz and the door swings open. He steps through it and I follow cautiously, with Nathan behind me.

"Welcome to Langford House," Scott says grandly, as I gape wordlessly. We're standing in a brightly lit, wide hallway with laminated flooring and exquisite wooden panelling. A counter takes up half the length of one wall, and behind it sits older woman, prim and proper in a pale grey suit, with pale hair styled short with loose curls, and wearing minimal make up. She's protected by what looks like some sort of bullet-proof glass – although truth be told it could just be perspex for all I would know. But somehow, I don't think they're the perspex type. She nods a greeting to Scott, who returns it, then she opens a hatch in the glass and passes through a small electronic pad. Scott crosses to her, his shoes clicking on the laminate flooring, and holds his hand on the pad, palm down. It beeps and he passes it back through. I guess it's some sort of identification scanner. There's a lot of security here, which is my experience is rarely a good thing.

The door slams shut with a bang and I jump, spinning around. Nathan raises his hands and offers an apologetic smile.

"Sorry."

My eyes have already slid past him though, onto the stoic man standing silently beside the door. He's wearing black shoes and a suit which doesn't completely cover the tattoo rising up onto his neck, but that's not what I'm staring at. It's the ugly black pistol at his hip that has my attention. I've never seen a gun in real life, and I barely suppress a shudder. It's a vicious-looking weapon, designed for just one purpose.

Nathan coughs discreetly and a figure appears by my side. I gasp and spin around, but it's just Scott, and he's showing me his empty hands.

"It's okay," he promises, and then shifts his gaze to the armed guard. "If Miss Mason here wants to leave at any time, you're to let her, understand?"

The man nods.

"And if I try to stop her," he adds as an afterthought, "feel free to shoot me."

"Yes, sir," the guard says, a smile twitching at the corners of his mouth.

I shake my head. I'm glad they think it's funny.

"Pay no attention, dear," the woman behind the counter says with a kindly smile. "They're like overgrown boys sometimes."

I smile back uncertainly, and behind me Nathan chuckles quietly at the reprimand.

"Alright, let's go," Scott says, and I'm feeling a little less tense as we approach another door out of the hallway. The woman presses another button behind the counter and the door slides to one side, revealing a lift. The three of us step into the confined space. The door slides shut, locking me inside the sterile box, with the powerfully built men standing guard on either side of me. Panic flutters in my throat, but I bury it quickly and set my jaw. I'm doing this. Scott presses a button marked 'basement' and the lift starts its descent. A few moments later it stops, and the doors open again.

"I'll check in with Gardiner," Nathan says, making no move to exit the lift. Scott nods and steps through the door, motioning for me to follow. We're in a hallway that seems too vast to belong to just the building we entered. I wonder if AbGen bought up the surrounding buildings to build below them.

We stop outside one of the doors, and Scott pulls out a card and swipes it through the reader. There's a soft click as the lock disengages. I want to ask what's on the other side of the door, but my throat is closing up. I'm starting to feel like a goldfish that's just been dumped in a fishing lake – I'm so far out of my depth that it would be laughable, if I wasn't so terrified. I close my eyes for a moment and take a breath. I'm here by choice. I want this.

Scott is standing patiently, watching me. He makes no move to rush me, even though this must be everyday stuff to him, and I must look like I'm completely overreacting. Maybe I am. This is just like walking into any other office, anywhere in the world. I nod to him and we walk through the door.

And it's not like any other office. To start with, it's not actually an office, more like some sort of gym. The room is spacious in a way that reminds me vaguely of a high school sports hall, with the high ceiling and wooden panels, but without any of the usual equipment. There's some kind of padded matting lining the floor, and a number of markings running along it that mean nothing to me. There are a few punch bags and a couple of treadmills against one wall, but the rest of the room is empty. Bright lighting shines down from the ceiling, and it would be easy to forget that I'm underground, except for the lack of windows, which gives the whole room an eerie feel.

There are two people wearing loose-fitting workout clothes in the centre of the room, sparring. They seem to be equally matched, and it's not until we get closer I notice one of them is a woman. Her sparring partner aims a punch at her throat, and she takes a quick half step to the side, then catches his arm as it reaches the space she had occupied moments before. A quick twist puts her behind her partner, and she pulls his arm up while pushing her foot into the back of his knee, sending him crashing to the floor. She keeps her hold on his arm, pinning him to the ground. Panting, she pauses a moment, a smile creeping onto her face, but before she has a chance to celebrate her victory, she is flying through the air and slamming into the mat. I wince in sympathy. Her partner somehow reversed her grip on his arm, too quickly even for me to see. He drops onto his knees, straddling her. He throws a punch at her throat but stops short.

"Never relax until your target is completely disabled," he tells her, getting to his feet. He offers her his hand and pulls her up. She covers the front of her right fist with the palm of her left hand and bows slightly, and he repeats the gesture back to her. She heads towards the door we've just come in through, nodding to us on her way past. Her sparring partner approaches us and greets Scott with a wide smile.

"Scott, how're you doing? Don't suppose you've come to spar?"

Scott plucks at his suit lapel with one hand.

"Not today."

"Excuses, excuses," the man says, shaking his head in mock disappointment, reaching for a sweat rag. Scott picks up a bottle of water and tosses it to him, and the man squirts some into his mouth.

"So, are you going to introduce us?" he asks, glancing in my direction.

"This is Anna. She's talented. Anna, meet Nick. He's one of our self-defence instructors."

"Good to meet you," Nick says, offering his hand. I shake it and repeat the sentiment.

"You must be looking for Paul, then?" he asks Scott.

"Have you seen him?"

Nick shakes his head.

"Try the comms room," he suggests.

Scott thanks him and we leave through the same door we came in.

"You're quiet," Scott says as we walk along the hallway.

"It's a lot to take in," I say. He nods his understanding.

"It was much smaller when I signed up. Pretty much none of the subterranean rooms existed then."

"How long ago was that?" It's hard to think of him being in my position at some stage. He seems pretty at home to me.

"Seven years, give or take. A lot's changed in that time. For the better."

We've reached another unmarked door with a card reader beside it. Scott swipes his card and we walk through. The contrast between this room and the last couldn't be greater. Though small, the room is packed with desks and computers. The walls are covered in charts, and there are several whiteboards with information jotted on them in various colour inks. At three of the computers, people are sitting, tapping away at the keyboards. Each is wearing a headset, and one person is speaking into his in muted tones.

Two more people are standing in front of one of the charts, and Scott strides across the carpet towards them with me trailing in his wake like a lost puppy. One is a man, perhaps late thirties, wearing the obligatory suit and sharp tie, with slightly thinning hair that he makes up for with stubble on his chin. His face is creased with lines that deepen when he frowns.

The person he's speaking to is a woman, who I would place in her mid to late twenties. She's wearing a well-cut matching suit jacket and skirt, which sits a little way above her knee, and a pair of heels that look too high to be practical in an office, although she balances on them with ease. Her blonde hair is shoulder-length and perfectly straight. It frames her face, accentuating her high cheekbones and contrasting with her brown eyes. Her make up is applied expertly and is the full works – right down to the mascara on curled lashes, and not-quite-natural shade of lipstick. The effect is striking, and I can't help but feel inadequate besides her. With her heels, she's several inches taller than me and she has a face and figure that would turn heads, and a confidence that suggests she knows it.

By contrast, my hair is a mess after waking up on wet grass, my clothes are slightly grubby and consist of jeans and a loose-fitting top, and my trainers are still covered in mud from the playing field. My makeup is virtually non-existent, and even with all the brushes and powders in the world, I could never re-create the masterpiece that is her face. I'm starting to wish I'd taken the time to tidy myself up before leaving with Scott. *Get a grip*, I tell myself. It's not like I even knew I was going to go with him until thirty seconds before I did it. There was hardly time for a makeover, and frankly, I've got bigger things to worry about right now.

The woman turns to me and smiles. Not the arrogant, condescending smile I expected, but a genuine, warm expression. I relax and start to feel a little less intimidated by her appearance. It's weird, because nothing has changed – she is still immaculately presented, and I still look like something the cat dragged in – but the contrast bothers me less. Or more precisely, she bothers me less. I can feel my emotions changing, like frozen hands thawing in front of a campfire, and I feel myself drawn to her, like I've finally found the one person who can give me the warmth and safety I've been seeking since this whole crazy mess began.

"Anna, this is Helen," Scott introduces us. "She can influence people's perception of her."

His words break me from her thrall, and I crash back into reality with a painful thud. It wasn't real. She's just a person, and there is no safety.

"So you're the new absa?" she says, scrutinising me. I look to Scott and raise an eyebrow.

"It stands for atypically biologically selectively advantaged," he explains. "That's what happens when you let scientists name things."

I turn the words over in my mind and open my mouth.

"She's in denial," he tells Helen, before I can deny it. I snap my mouth shut again. Helen nods knowingly.

"Trust me, you're not the first. But Scott's talent has never let him down yet."

I turn to Scott in surprise.

61

"You're an… absa?"

He presses his lips together and Helen's face falls.

"I'm sorry, you hadn't told her, had you?"

He shrugs and his lips settle into an easy smile again.

"It never came up."

I think my mouth may actually drop open. Never came up? That's just… I regain control of my lower jaw and force a smile to match his.

"So, what can you do?"

"I'm a tracker," he says, the careful look back in his eyes. "That's how I knew you were one of us."

One of us. I like the sound of that. But what exactly am I getting myself into? My eyes have drifted past him to the whiteboard behind him. His eyes follow mine and he raises a hand placatingly.

"I can explain."

"Really? Because it looks a lot like you've been spying on me," I snap. The whiteboard is covered in photos – CCTV from the jewellers, me walking down the street, me at The Glasshouse. And details – my entire life written in dry wipe marker. Date of birth, habits, everywhere I've lived, everyone I know. My eyes roam over it, taking it all in.

"Anna, this is a top-secret organisation. We wanted to help you, but we had no way of knowing if you needed our help."

"You could have asked."

"I tried, remember?"

Remember? How could I not? I'm pretty sure I will be taking that particular memory to the grave. A stranger turning up at my door and sending me shifting twenty miles away isn't the sort of thing you just forget. I sigh.

"I'm being unfair."

"You're being honest, and I'm glad you trust me enough to do that. I don't blame you for being spooked." He gestures to the board. "On the plus side, we don't need this anymore."

"Good." I barely suppress a shudder as I eye the board again, and then turn my back on it. Helen and her companion are watching me unobtrusively.

"Don't worry, it scared the hell out of me when I first got here too," Helen says. "You get used to it."

I nod, unconvinced. I'm not sure this is something I want to get used to – any of it. Scott has fallen into conversation with Helen's companion, and they've moved a few steps away. It doesn't take a genius to work out who they're talking about.

"Who's he?" I ask Helen, surprising myself with my directness. Normally I have better manners. There's definitely something off about the way I'm acting around her. If Helen is bothered by my boldness, she doesn't let on.

"That's Paul. He's in charge of damage limitation."

"Damage limitation?" I frown.

"Yeah. It's his job to make sure what we do here stays secret. Like when someone disappears in front of two cops, or in the middle of a restaurant." She laughs lightly and I chuckle too – though I have no idea why. Nothing about this is remotely funny. But it feels good to laugh, and before I know it, the pair of us are in fits of giggles over nothing.

Scott makes his way back over with a bemused smile.

"I'm glad to see you girls are getting along. Care to share the joke?"

"It's nothing," Helen says, her laugher fading smile. "I'll catch up with you two later."

*

"Okay, we've got one last call to make."

I attempt to suppress a yawn but it's a lost cause so I give up the fight, and fix Scott with an unimpressed stare.

"Seriously? It's–" I check the time on my signal-less phone, "–nine p.m. Can't it wait?"

He looks pained. I sigh in exasperation.

"Fine. But I need a coffee. Who are we meeting?"

"My boss."

A cold shudder runs through me, and I remember the whiteboard in the comms room. This is the man who made it his mission to find out everything about me, the man who sent Scott to see if I could do this thing they thought I could. Hell, the man who runs all of this, who *controls* all of this. A man like that could make me disappear if he wanted.

"Just relax," Scott tells me, and I realise I'm breathing like a racehorse. But on the plus side, I haven't blacked out, or shifted, or whatever. "It's nothing formal, just a chat. And you can still leave if you want to. But–" He rubs his hand over his face, and the stress makes him look older. The stress of dealing with me.

"Stop. I get it." I sigh again. "But just so you know, if he tries to chain me up in the basement, I'm holding you personally responsible."

He laughs.

"Right, got it."

I follow him back into the lift, and he presses the button for the top floor. I try to focus on my breathing. The fact that I'm too tired to be properly afraid is definitely helping. Whatever's coming, I have to see it through. And I think I can trust these people. Or Scott, at least. He went through the same thing as me and, well, I guess in a way he seems less strange to me now. Like we're part of the same thing, and the same thing is part of us. Only that sounds ridiculous. Must be the exhaustion catching up to me. I really could use a coffee, but Scott thinks I'm twitchy enough already, and that caffeine is a bad idea. He's probably right.

The lift rumbles to a stop, and the door slides slowly open. I step through it on shaking legs, and jump as a hand lands on my shoulder. Scott gives it a reassuring squeeze.

"Just take your time, we're in no hurry."

I nod and stretch out my hand against the wall to steady myself. This is no big deal. He's just a man. After everything I've been through in the last two days, this is child's play. Or he could be planning on locking me up in the research department. You know, one or the other.

"Okay, let's get it over with before I change my mind."

He smiles and leads me down the corridor. We reach a large imposing door – or maybe it just seems that way to me, knowing what it symbolises. Scott knocks on it twice, and flashes me another reassuring smile. All the smiling is making me kinda edgy, but I don't have time to dwell on it. A voice from inside the room instructs us to enter. Scott swings the door open and gestures for me to go through. I step meekly, looking around as I do.

The room is carpeted with thick burgundy flooring, and the walls are half panelled, half painted a cream colour. A large mahogany desk dominates the room, which itself is larger than you would think necessary for an office. On the other hand, having never worked in an office, I guess I'm hardly best placed to judge.

Behind the desk sits another suit, though even from my inexperienced perspective I can tell that this one must have cost a fortune. The guy wearing it is older, late fifties perhaps, white-haired but still in good shape. Though he's sitting behind a desk now, I get the impression that he's no stranger to a day's work. His eyes are grey, and they're watching me closely in a way that makes me feel like a mouse crossing a snake's path. I feel a shudder working its way up my spine.

He rises from his seat with a smile that doesn't reach his eyes as Scott shuts the door, and steps from behind his desk.

"You must be Anna," he says, stretching out his hand towards me. "Issac Gardiner."

I take a step backwards and bump into Scott.

"She's a little jittery right now," he says over my shoulder.

Jittery? Yeah, I suppose I am, but who wouldn't be? Two days ago, I was a waitress whose biggest worry was being behind on her rent. Now I'm a thief, a wanted criminal, and a genetic mutant for crying out loud. Oh yeah, and the government are trying to recruit me to do God alone knows what. So yeah, I'm jittery. Sue me. Or lock me in a laboratory.

"I understand," Gardiner says, his smile not faltering for a moment. His hand drops back to his side and he perches on the edge of his desk, which just looks plain weird for a guy his age.

"So, what do you think of our little facility, Miss Mason?"

"It's... um..." Creepy? Clandestine? Terrifying? "Nice."

"We have one of the best labs in the world here, and some of the top researchers. Our training facilities are second to none."

I try to rephrase my appraisal into something more flattering, but he holds up his hand to stop me.

"I'm not fishing for compliments, Miss Mason – may I call you Anna? – I just want you to know what we can offer you, should you decide to come on board. Scott tells me you've been experiencing some unfortunate side effects as a result of using your talent."

"He has?" I glance at him over my shoulder, and then turn back to Gardiner. I fight down the illogical panic that's rising to the surface again, because what have I really got to panic about? I mean, okay, he knows more about me than I'm comfortable with, but of course Scott was going to report back to him – the man's his boss. And since when was Scott my emotional crutch, anyway? He was the one I didn't trust this morning.

68

"I know it's late, so I'll keep this short," he continues. "We could use someone with your ability. And you could use an organisation with our resources. Helping you gain control of your talent is just the start of what we could offer you."

"And what would you want in return?" I manage to force out.

He chuckles, and my frown deepens.

"I'm offering you a job; nothing more, nothing less. Scott can give you an idea of what it entails. Take some time, sleep on it. But let me know soon."

He rises from his perch and moves back behind the desk. I guess we're dismissed. I follow Scott from the office, Gardiner's words running through my mind. A job working for the shady government organisation? I don't know what scares me more: that they want me, or that I'm actually considering it.

"Anna?" Scott has stopped and is looking at me expectantly.

"I'm sorry, did you say something?"

"Did you want to sleep here tonight, or do you want me to take you home?"

Shady government organisation and B&B service – the surprises just keep on coming.

"Home, please."

He nods and glances at his watch.

"It'll be late by the time you get back; we can eat first if you want?"

I hesitate. I haven't eaten all day thanks to Scott showing up at the restaurant and my defence mechanism helpfully sending me twenty miles across town. Even so, I'll be much happier once I'm out of here. This whole place makes me feel uneasy. Scott picks up on my indecision and makes it easy for me.

"We'll grab something on the way. Come on."

Chapter Six

The harsh lighting is a sharp contrast to the heavy darkness outside the large glass windows. I'm sitting on a red plastic chair, at a white laminated table – the sort favoured by service stations up and down the country, and that are all too familiar to me. That's the price you pay for having a mother with an aversion to staying in one place for too long. Just looking around brings back the exhaustion of all those long childhood journeys.

I lift my coffee cup and take a sip, glancing round the almost-deserted service station restaurant. A couple are cuddled up together on the other side of the room, and closer to us a man is drinking from a coffee and catching up on his text messages. We're tucked away in a quiet corner at a table Scott picked. Something to do with being able to see all the doors and the other diners. I'm sure it made sense to him. I just want to get something to eat and get home. He has other things on his mind, though. I lower the cup back to the table and consider his question. He wants to know how I'd feel about accepting AbGen's help.

"I don't know. I've got so many questions – I don't even know what you guys do, not really."

"There's a limit to how much I can tell you," he says, his face staying carefully stoic. "AbGen operates outside of the public eye. It has to, for our own protection."

That makes sense. I hadn't really thought about it – it's not like I've had much time to sit and think – but if people knew what we could do, they would panic. Maybe want to lock me in a cage and do all the things I was worried about Gardiner doing to me. We're different. People would fear us; we would be the enemy. So I understand the need for secrecy. Doesn't mean I'm willing to jump in blindly.

"What are you allowed to tell me?"

Scott adds another teaspoon of sugar to his coffee and stirs it, then removes the spoon and sets it on the edge of his saucer.

"We spend a lot of our time in training, making the most of the facilities you saw today."

Training for what? I want to ask him, but I bite my tongue and wait with as much patience as I can muster while he takes a sip from his cup.

"Our scientists are doing research into why our genetic makeup is different and how it gives us our abilities. But I'm guessing you're not too interested in that. The work we do is varied. I know it sounds clichéd, but we do whatever is needed. Sometimes our work is international, sometimes we're on our own streets.

72

AbGen is about saving people. As for how we do that, well, it depends on your talent."

A waitress brings over two plates of food and smiles at Scott – ignoring me – as she sets them down on the table. I stare at the plate in front of me while she busies herself setting down cutlery, thinking about how Scott has managed to use a lot of words to tell me precisely nothing. The waitress asks if we want refills on our drinks and finally leaves when we decline. I pick up my fork and poke at my chicken salad, not as hungry as I was half an hour ago.

"And this work that you're being so cryptic about," I probe. "Is it dangerous?"

"It can be," he answers, surprising me with his honesty. I'll admit it, I'm a little impressed, too. If he was going to lie to me, that was the obvious question to dodge.

"But we have good back-up, and we never go into a situation blind. I'll be honest with you, Anna, there are risks involved, but the work we do saves lives, and I think it's worth it. You need to decide if you do too."

I nod, and wipe a round of cucumber through some salad dressing. I'm not the walking into danger type, I think the last two days prove that – I've spent pretty much the entire time running, freaking out, or both. I can see the way Scott's eyes come alive when he speaks about the work they do. He really believes in what he's doing, but that's hardly justification enough for me to join him taking these undisclosed risks for some elusive greater good.

"You have a firing range – would I be expected to–" The waitress walks past, and I lower my voice, "–kill anyone?"

"We're not assassins," he says. "We carry guns for defensive purposes. But if we need to use them, then we're authorised to do so."

I nod as if people tell me this sort of thing every day and try to keep my heart rate somewhere south of a hundred beats a minute.

"And how would it work? I turn up for work on Monday and Gardiner sends me off somewhere with a gun and a radio?"

"Well, like I said, we spend most of our time training, and you'd need a lot of training before he made you operational. There's no way of telling how long it would take you to get control of your ability. But once you do, you'd be fully briefed before being sent anywhere, and you'd have a handler watching your back the entire time. Oh, and we don't use radios; they tend to be a bit conspicuous."

He takes another sip of his coffee and watches me with amused eyes. But something he's said has caught my attention.

"A handler?"

"That's right. You'd be assigned an agent whose job is to make sure you're fully briefed, and keep you safe."

"Who would it be?"

He shakes his head.

"I don't know. That's for Gardiner to decide."

I chew a piece of lettuce and force myself to swallow, whilst resolving to eat around the rest of it. It turns out ruining a salad is easier than I imagined.

"And I'd be working from the base most of the time?"

"It's not exactly a nine-to-five job, but you'd be expected to log a certain number of training hours each week. We could sort you out with a car, or get you a flat closer to the base."

"I have a car."

"One that works," he clarifies with a smile. I put my fork down.

"Do you have any idea how creepy it is that you know so much about me? Any idea at all? Is there anything you don't know?"

"I don't know why you sold your motorbike to buy a car that doesn't work."

I laugh despite myself. I'd loved that bike. Maybe a little too much. I'd particularly liked how fast it could go – until I got caught doing ninety-five in a fifty zone. I came within a whisker of losing my license, and decided I needed something that was less likely to tempt me to test the speed cameras. Of course, the car had been working when I bought it... just not for long afterwards. Just long enough, in fact, for the warranty to run out.

"What's the pay like?" I'm not considering it, not really, but there's no harm in asking, right?

"At least ten times what you get now. More, if you're on an assignment."

On the other hand, maybe I should consider it.

"Give it some thought – sleep on it. Gardiner doesn't expect a decision right now, and you've had one hell of a day. But when you make up your mind, give me a call."

He slides a business card across the table to me. It has just his first name and phone number printed on the plain white card. I pick it up and slide it into my pocket.

"Yeah, I'll do that."

*

When the alarm wakes me from my restless sleep the next morning, I wonder if the entire thing was a dream, and then I roll over onto my side and see the business card lying next to my lamp. I yawn and burrow further into the duvet, but don't take my eyes from the card. It all seems so surreal.

I spent half the night thinking about Gardiner's offer, and everything Scott told me about AbGen, which admittedly isn't much. But it's enough to make me question my future at The Glasshouse. Until now I've been content to plod along, one pay cheque at a time, carving out a little niche for myself in an anonymous town. And I like my niche. But now Scott has me wondering if I'm missing out on something more. The passion I'd seen in his eyes last night, the sense of purpose, of belonging. And I can't deny that it was flattering that they'd gone to so much trouble to recruit me: I've never been head-hunted before. It's not like there's a dire shortage of averagely skilled waitresses.

But he'd made no bones about the fact that it could be dangerous. What would I do if someone tried to kill me? Worse, how would I cope if I had to kill someone? I feel guilty if I get someone's order wrong at the restaurant, which sort of pales in significance to what AbGen might ask of me.

The money, yes, that's a pretty big deal. As a waitress, I can generally make ends meet – if you don't count the slight cash flow problem I've been having for the last couple of months – but the sort of money Scott was talking about would make a real difference. If I'm still around to spend it.

I sit up and push the duvet off, shivering as the cold air raises goose-bumps on my skin. What it comes down to is trust. Do I trust Scott? Yes, I think so. He's been pretty honest with me so far, and he's kept all his promises. But do I trust Gardiner? Not in a million years. The way he looked at me yesterday made my skin crawl. Like I was some sort of prize racehorse. He wants my talent, but I have no idea what for – or how far he's willing to go to get it.

I shake my head and swing my legs off the bed. I'm being paranoid. Like I said, family trait. They let me leave yesterday, and they could have stopped me – it's not like I have anything close to control over my ability. They've made it clear this is my choice.

I'm going round in circles. I spent half the night worrying about the same issues, and I'd hoped some sleep would clear my head. So much for that.

I step into the shower and let the warm water wash over my body, giving myself over entirely to the relaxing sensation. The scent of ylang ylang and roses hangs in the steamy air, joined by honey blossom as I shampoo my hair. The morning ritual makes me feel halfway human again, and by the time I'm dressed I'm ready to make a couple of calls.

The first is to Lloyd. I put on my best croaky voice and tell him I can't make it in today. I feel horrible lying to him, but I'm sure Janey will appreciate the extra hours, and I have somewhere I need to be.

The second is to Janey herself. If Lloyd tells her I called in sick after everything we spoke about two days ago, she's going to panic. I owe her some sort of explanation, not that I've got any idea what I'm going to tell her. *Hey, Janey, it's okay, it turns out I'm a mutant with super-powers and the government wants to recruit me!* Yeah, that conversation would go well. I mean, depending on how you feel about men in white coats.

"Anna, how are you?" she answers almost before it's had time to ring. "I was getting worried when you didn't call."

"I know," I say, grimacing. "I'm sorry. Things got a little crazy."

"But you're okay?"

"I'm okay. And I've been talking to someone about my… blackouts." I hope she doesn't notice my hesitation. I want to tell her everything, of course, but I can't drag her into the middle of this.

"And?"

"He's got some theories. They're going to run some tests." Though probably not the sort of tests Janey expects. I hate this! I hate that I can't be honest with her.

Maybe I should just tell her anyway. I mean, she's my best friend. She'd understand, right? Right, and then what? Scott was pretty clear about AbGen being some sort of national secret. Until I know more about them, I can't tell anyone. Especially not Janey. And there's only one way I can find out. "I'm going to call him in a minute."

"Anna Mason, are you stalling?"

"Well, maybe just a little," I confess.

"Don't think I'm going to sit here being your enabler," she says, her voice playful. "I'm going to hang up now, and you can fill me in tonight, at my place, got it?"

"Got it." The prospect of a girly night puts a smile on my face – though it falters a little when I realise she's going to want answers that I won't be able to give.

"And Anna? Call him. I'm serious."

The line goes dead. I pull the phone away from my ear, take a deep breath, and then dial again.

The electronic ringing sounds in my ear for a long moment before Scott picks up.

"Hello."

I wonder if not identifying himself is a security thing, or if he just has really bad telephone manners.

"Hi, it's me." Two can play at that game. I smile to myself, and then let the expression fall away. "Can we talk?"

"Yeah. Meet me at Arundel Corner in an hour."

The line goes dead and I kick around the flat for as long as I can stomach before grabbing my coat and heading for the door. I get to the Arundel Corner early, and loiter on the street, trying hard not to look too obvious as I watch the traffic coming and going, looking for Scott's car. I thrust my hands into my pockets and lean back against the wall, enjoying the sun warming my skin. This is a definite improvement on the damp greyness of yesterday.

The occasional car drives past, but none that I recognise. An engine snarls and a shiver runs through me. I recognise the sounds of a well-tuned bike. I miss the freedom of racing along the tarmac, chasing a sequence of white lines that lead to some place in the distance that matters less than the journey. Cars are okay, and they have their perks – heaters, for one thing – but they're too confining, too restrictive. A bike is like an extension of your body, but in a car, your body is just an extension of the vehicle.

The snarling eases to a rumble as the bike – a big, shining black beast – slows, and the rider looks around. It's a Suzuki Bandit, an elegant machine that looks the part and performs even better. I've always loved the design of the machine, big brother to the Suzuki EN, the first bike I'd ever ridden. The rider looks straight at me, though I only vaguely register it because I'm still too busy eyeing up his machine, and wondering if I can get credit for one.

The bike eases across the road and idles beside me. Its rider pulls off his helmet, and I do a double take. It's Scott, but I hadn't figured him for the biker type. You know, in case it messed up his suit. He's wearing full leathers, gloves and boots, and has a second helmet at his elbow, with his arm pushed through it. He pulls it off and passes it to me with a smile.

"What are you waiting for?"

I grin and pull it on, then hop onto the back of the bike. There's no pillion grab bar – which must be a customisation, as the standard model comes with one – so I wrap my arms around his waist.

"Hang on," he calls as he clips his helmet back into place, and then revs the engine. The bike shudders in anticipation and then we pull away, changing gear twice before we hit the corner, and then twice more once we round it. I see now why he chose Arundel – we're straight onto the back roads to Ryebridge, and we both know there are no speed cameras around here.

The lane is deserted, just a grey expanse, and trees whip past on either side of us. Scott leans the bike and takes us smoothly through a wide corner, and I concede he's a good rider. Which is good, because there is nothing more terrifying than being on the back of someone's bike when that someone can't ride. Not even Gardiner's laboratory.

I settle down and enjoy the ride, laughing with exhilaration as Scott kicks it up a notch. I peer over his shoulder and see we're clocking way above a tonne. I guess stripping off the pillion bar wasn't his only customisation. The wind snatches away my laughter and the scream of the bike makes any sort of conversation impossible, leaving us isolated in the moment, connected only through the touch of my arms at his waist. My every thought is drowned out by the noise, so that I'm completely in the moment, with no thought of what happened yesterday or might happen tomorrow. Nothing more than just the next three seconds, and the next, and the next.

The bike vibrates beneath us, trembling with its raw power as we roar across the tarmac. I've lost all track of where we are, and I don't care.

Scott eases off the throttle and kicks it down a gear. We're passing a trickle of traffic travelling in the opposite direction to us, and I suppose we must be joining the main roads again soon. I'm wrong, though.

We swing round a sweeping bend, and then a tight one in the opposite direction, and Scott slows the bike to a crawl. The smooth tarmac turns to loose stones that crunch under the bike's wheels, and then to mud. I look around me and see green hills overlooking a wide lake whose water glistens in the sunlight. Scott kills the engine and I hear birds crying as they circle over-head and swoop periodically at the water. It couldn't be more different to where we'd come from.

I climb off the bike and pull the helmet from my head.

"It's beautiful."

"I like to come out here to think," he tells me, pulling off his own helmet and gloves. I can see why. It's so peaceful, so tranquil. It's a world away from the crashing waves of the Essex coast that had been my getaway when things got too much. There's something about water, though, whether calm or turbulent, that has a soothing effect on the soul. Or so my meditation teacher told me. I'm starting to think she may have been on to something – and if anyone's soul could use a little soothing right about now, it's mine.

"What?" Scott asks, catching my smile. I sit back on the grassy bank and tell him about the coast, though I don't tell him about the hours I spent screaming into the wind because I figure that might give him the wrong impression about my sanity.

"This is much more peaceful," I conclude.

"I thought peaceful might do you some good, after the weekend you've had," he says, picking up a stone and skimming it across the surface of the lake. "Although I don't know how I'd have explained it to Gardiner if you'd shifted right off the back of the bike," he adds with a frown.

I lie back on the ground and stare up at the clouds drifting across the blue sky.

"Do you ever regret joining AbGen?" I ask him.

"Never."

"You don't get sick of all the training, or worry about the danger when you're on an assignment?"

"The training prepares you for the danger, so it takes a lot of the risk out of it. Training might not be exciting, but when you think of it in those terms, you don't mind doing it. Everyone feels a little fear when they start going on assignments – that's natural – but most of the time there's very little danger involved. Our training prepares us for every eventuality."

I mull that over for a moment, and it makes sense. I'm not really a gym person, and nothing appeals to me about running through the streets in the sweltering summer or freezing winter, but if I was training for a reason then I'd probably be a bit more enthusiastic about it. And I can't deny that I get a little thrill of excitement when I think about learning to control my talent. It turns to anxiety when I think back to the way Gardiner looked at me yesterday.

"And do you ever worry..." I hesitate, not sure if asking is the smart thing to do. Subterranean offices and firing ranges, highly trained agents on secret missions... that's a lot of power for one person to wield, especially when that one person is an aging guy in a suit who sends chills down my spine, in the bad way. Scott is looking at me curiously, his expression open and eyes non-judgemental. "How do you know you're working for the right side?"

He treats the question with the seriousness I intended it, not trying to laugh it off or change the subject, which I figure is a good sign. I sit up and look at him properly.

"When Gardiner recruited me, AbGen was much smaller, just a handful of people. I was one of the first absas and I didn't understand what was happening to me. A lot like you, actually. He took me into his office and offered me a job, and I asked him the same question. He told me that humanity is hard-wired to believe it's in the right, and our perception of justice is skewed by wherever we're standing at the time. Every dictator throughout history has believed that they're serving the greater good, and even Jihadists believe that they're serving a higher calling by cleansing the world of infidels. So no-one can answer that question for you. We have to judge ourselves by our actions, and hold ourselves accountable to a higher standard. We have to fight to protect our way of life, and preserve the lives of as many as we can. At AbGen, that's what we do. We protect people. We protect their freedom."

I nod, turning the words over in my head. If we all believe we're right, all the time, then it's true: whatever we think is the greater good is a moot point. But if they're saving lives, not taking them, how bad can they be? And how can I walk away from the chance to be a part of that?

"Okay, I'm in."

Chapter Seven

By midday, I'm back at Langford House, waiting outside Gardiner's office like a naughty school kid while Scott speaks to him behind the closed door. I've agreed to sign on with AbGen, but I have one condition. There's no way I'm prepared to trust my safety to someone I've never met. I've told them I want Scott as my handler, or I'll walk. Gardiner has asked me to wait outside, and here I've sat for half an hour. I think Scott is trying to sell him on the idea, but the door is thick and it's impossible to make out what's being said. If I put my ear against it, I might be able to hear better, but that could be tricky to explain if someone happens to come down the corridor.

I fidget, getting uncomfortable on the chair. Maybe I've pushed things too far – misjudged Gardiner's desire to have access to my talent. Maybe he'd rather turn me away than have me laying down stipulations. Or maybe he's realising that he could just force me to do what he wants. My anxiety has been growing over the last thirty minutes, and I can feel my stress levels rising. *Don't shift, don't shift, don't shift*, I chant silently, which isn't helping, because now I'm panicking about shifting right out of the corridor, which is just making it more likely to happen.

I force myself to take a deep breath, and then another. It doesn't matter if Gardiner doesn't like it, because this is a deal breaker. If I can't have Scott as my handler then I'll gladly go back to waiting tables at The Glasshouse, and just as I'm starting to think that maybe I should have just stuck to that in the first place, the door swings open. Scott walks through and gives me a wink. Gardiner stands in the doorway. I scramble to my feet.

"You have yourself a job, Miss Mason," he says, extending his hand to me. I shake it and try to remind myself that he's one of the good guys.

Scott leads me to the lift, and presses a button marked 'Lower Basement'.

"What's down there?" I ask him.

"Promise me you're not going to panic and shift."

"I promise nothing," I warn, eyeing him suspiciously, but I've stuck it out this long. I've got no intention of going anywhere, not if I can help it.

"We're going to the labs. Gardiner wants you to see our scientists, and one of the doctors, to see if they can get to the bottom of what's causing your blackouts."

"Right." I nod, and sag against the back wall of the lift. The scientists. The lab. Tests.

"You can trust us, Anna," Scott says softly. I look at him and he holds my eye, locking me in the moment.

"They just want to help, and I won't let anything happen to you."

I nod again, but before I can reply, the door rolls open. The lift opens directly into the lab, which is vast, easily the biggest room I have seen at Langford House so far. The whitewashed walls and white tiled floors give the place a sterile feel, and it's spotless to a fault. Men in white lab coats are working at computers and checking readouts from a hundred pieces of equipment that wouldn't have looked out of place aboard the Enterprise. Harsh lighting reflects off the stainless steel lab tables. I don't see any scalpels or restraints, which is something, at least.

Sensing my hesitation, Scott touches my elbow and raises an eyebrow.

"Ready?"

My mouth is dry, and my answer comes out as a croak. I moisten my lips and try again.

"Yes."

He walks from the lift and I follow a step behind. Our footsteps echo across the tiles; his confident, mine hesitant, as we approach an older man in a white lab coat, with wiry white hair and deep laughter lines set into his face. He rises from his seat to greet Scott with a handshake and me with a kindly smile.

"Anna, this is Doctor Pearce," Scott introduces us. "Doc, this is Anna."

"It's lovely to meet you, dear," the doctor says, making no attempt to touch me, for which I'm grateful. He's not what I imagined, not by a long shot. I'd been envisioning something more along the lines of the mad professor, syringe in hand, working in a dark laboratory-cum-dungeon. I much prefer the lab I'm standing in to the one in my over-active imagination.

"And you," I manage, attempting a smile in response.

"You flatter me. I know you youngsters have a hundred places you'd rather be than in my little lab." His eyes crinkle with mirth and I find myself relaxing.

"Walter is the head scientist here," Scott explains.

"I won't take up any more of your time than is strictly necessary, dear," Walter promises, and gestures to a chair beside one of the stainless steel tables. "Would you be so kind as to sit?"

I lower myself into the chair, with a nervous glance at Scott and then back at Walter. My heart is racing, but dread is loosening its stranglehold on my gut. Walter places a voice recorder on the table between us and eases into the chair opposite me. Scott chooses not to sit, instead standing by my shoulder. There's something reassuring about his presence.

"I'm afraid my memory's not what it used to be," the scientist tells me with a smile, and presses the machine's record button. I catch myself about to chew my nails and thrust my hands into my lap, and wait for him to begin his questions.

"When was the first time you became aware of your talent?"

"On Saturday," I tell him. "At the shopping centre."

"Could you tell me what exactly you can do, in your own words?"

"I'm... not really sure. I black out." I hesitate, and Walter nods his encouragement. "And I wake up somewhere else."

"And do you have any control over when it happens, or where you awaken?"

I shake my head.

"It happens when I get scared, I never know when it's going to happen or where I'm going to end up."

"That must be quite a terrifying experience," he says. "We'll see what we can do to help you understand how to control it."

"That would be good," I venture, which is the understatement of the year. Getting a handle on this craziness would be a huge relief.

In the end, Walter questions me for the best part of an hour – what's the furthest I've travelled, what was the last thing I was thinking before each time I shifted, what was the first thing I thought when I woke up. I answer honestly and in as much detail as I can, even when things get personal. I'm not sure how relevant my absentee father is, nor the fact that we moved homes twelve times in eight years when I was a kid, but frankly I'd tell him my bra size if he thought for one moment it would help. He doesn't ask, in case you're wondering. Finally, he reaches over and switches off the recorder.

"Thank you for your time," he says, and rises to his feet with an audible click from his knees. I get up, blinking in surprise.

"That's it? No tests, or...?"

"Doctor Maynard will take some blood for us to run tests on, but your answers will suffice for the time being. We'll need to speak to you again later."

"Thank you."

"You're most welcome, my dear."

I look at Scott, who is still standing in the same position he adopted at my shoulder, and from which he hasn't moved a muscle throughout the entire interview. I wonder if his legs have seized up from being immobile for so long. I can't sit still for more than a few minutes without fidgeting.

He leads me to the back of the lab, and I see a door set into the wall, with a plaque on it reading 'Medical'.

Scott taps twice on the door, and a voice from within invites us to enter. We do, and Scott shuts the door behind us. The room itself is quite small, with the same décor as the lab, and with the added odour of disinfectant. It reminds me of a hospital, but without the beds, nurses and patients, which seems like a strange comparison, but then it's a strange place. The single occupant sits behind a dark wooden desk which is taken up with a computer and keyboard. He wears a white doctor's coat, and has a stethoscope draped around his neck. He's younger than I expect, in his early thirties, with short dark hair and a serious expression.

"Ah, Scott, I was expecting you," he says as he rises to his feet, and then transfers his attention to me. "And you must be Miss Mason."

He doesn't seem to expect an answer so I don't give one, instead taking a moment to look around the room. Several framed certificates line the sterile white walls, listing the achievements and qualifications of one Doctor Maynard. They're the only personal touches to the entire room. A medical bed with a paper sheet is tucked against one wall, with a tray of equipment beside it. I don't look too closely at that. A door is set into the wall beside it, and I wonder where it leads. Maybe that's where the torture chamber is.

Scott coughs and looks pointedly at me.

"I'm sorry?"

"I said, please take a seat." Maynard is gesturing to the bed, so I hop up onto it, my feet dangling over the edge.

"Roll up your left sleeve."

I do so, feeling a vague sense of unease as he pulls on a pair of latex gloves and picks up a strip of rubber. He ties the tourniquet around my upper arm and instructs me to make a fist. I clench my hand, and he takes a swab, dips it into some disinfectant, and rubs it around the vein near my elbow. The cold liquid sends a shudder through me, though that has more to do with the knowledge of what's coming than the temperature of the disinfectant. I've spent years avoiding my doctor like the plague because he's overly fond of pricking me with needles, and somehow here I am, sitting on a medical trolley, waiting for yet another doctor to stick me without a single objection. Funny how life works.

He takes a syringe from an unopened packet and inspects the needle. Sadist. I turn my eyes away, staring over his shoulder. My eyes settle on Scott, who is watching me with a calm expression. I catch sight of the bike boots he didn't change from earlier, and smile. His Bandit is one hell of a machine. I replay the ride in my mind, the speed, the wind, the rush of adrenaline as the bike leaned low into the sweeping corners. The needle pricks my arm and I bite back a yelp as it slides into my vein and sucks up my blood like a tiny little vampire. I don't see how much he's taking, but he's taking his sweet time about it. It's not that it hurts – well, not much anyway – but the sight of the needle sticking into my arm creeps me out. It's not natural.

"Okay, that part's done," the doctor says, setting the needle down on a tray beside me. He gives me a small dressing to hold against the wound until the bleeding stops, then hands me a gown and directs me to a curtain.

"You can get changed behind there."

Changed? That's the first I've heard of this. Scott gives me a reassuring nod which fails to reassure, but I'm going to have to start trusting these people at some point. Might as well be now. I pick up the gown and walk behind the screen. I strip and pull on the gown, immediately feeling more vulnerable. I exhale slowly and step back into view, shuffling my bare feet across the tiles.

"Through here, please." Maynard holds open the door at the back of the room and I walk through. He turns to Scott.

"You'll need to wait out here."

I'm about to protest, but Maynard has already shut the door. My heart is thumping against my chest again and I can feel the blood pulsing in my fingertips. I need to get a grip. I'm supposed to be trusting him, and anyway, if Scott was worried, he would have insisted on sticking with me. But he didn't, because Maynard is a colleague of his – hell, a colleague of mine now – and, doctor or not, that means he can be trusted.

This room is much bigger than the last, and sectioned off by a number of green medical screens. Large diagnostic machines dominate most of the space – I vaguely recognise most of them from my former obsession with the TV show Casualty. I know, I know. For a girl who hated needles, I have strange taste. One of the machines is an MRI, and another is a CT scanner. There's an X-ray, too, and several pieces I don't recognise.

Maynard steers me towards the MRI. He asks me to lie back and hands me a small box with a button on it.

"The scan will take about half an hour. You'll need to lie very still. If you have a problem, press the button."

I lean my head back on the padded bench, and close my eyes, picturing the tranquil lake from earlier as the bench slides inside the machine.

Half an hour is a long time to lie completely still in an alien environment, when your entire world has been turned upside down in the last three days. You can get a lot of thinking done, which isn't necessarily a good thing, particularly when you're trying your damnedest not to freak out and shift half-way through the procedure.

Somehow I manage it though, and the bench eventually slides me back out into the bright lighting of the medical room. I sit up slowly and swing my legs over the side of the bench, stretching out the kinks in my muscles.

"What's next, doc?"

Chapter Eight

If I'd realised Maynard was going to take that as an invitation to run every test known to mankind, I would have phrased the question differently. It's several hours later when I finally trudge out of his office, letting the door swing shut behind me. AbGen's thorough, I'll give them that. The med wing was filled with more equipment than my local hospital, and Maynard had been on some sort of personal crusade to use each piece. I always knew doctors were sadists at heart.

I glance around the brightly lit laboratory filled with white-coated scientists attending industriously to their computers and charts, and my eyebrows knit together – there's no sign of Scott. He's obviously sloped off and abandoned me to my doctor-riddled fate.

"Traitor," I mutter, and notice the closest white coat giving me a funny look. Right. It's probably not normal to stand around talking to yourself. I duck my head and make a beeline for the lift doors before anyone can decide I need a psychiatric evaluation. Before I get there, the clicking of heels hurries across the tiled flooring behind me.

"Anna!"

I turn and see Helen hurrying towards me, and wait for her to catch up.

"Scott asked me to wait for you," she says. "He thought you'd want to see a friendly face after going through Maynard's tests."

"Yeah, thanks. Where is he, anyway?"

"Gardiner wanted to see him and Nathan. Come on, let's head over to the cafeteria. We can get a coffee while we wait for them."

We carry on walking towards the lift, and I watch as she presses her thumb against a small panel on the wall.

"What did Gardiner want?" I ask as the door slides open. We step inside and she presses a button on the display marked Upper Basement. The door rolls shut silently, and the lift slides smoothly into motion.

"You threw a bit of a spanner in the works when you asked for Scott as your handler," she says with a smile. "After all, where does that leave *his* handler?"

"Oh." I frown. I hadn't thought of that. In fact, it hadn't even occurred to me that Nathan was his handler. I guess I'd imagined the handler-absa relationship a little differently to what I'd seen between them.

"Don't worry," she says as we exit the lift into a long corridor lined with doors. "They'll work something out. Gardiner was pretty keen to have you on the team."

"Why?"

She chuckles as she pushes open the first door we come to.

"You're the ultimate spy, Anna. There's nowhere you can't go, and all without passing a single person."

I consider that as I glance around the cafeteria – it looks like any canteen the world over, if you ignored the lack of windows – and hope the shudder that runs through me isn't too obvious. Spying on who? I bury the thought. I'm committed now. And anyway, I want to be here. I want to help. At a couple of the tables we pass a few people sit in conversation, but most of them are empty. There's a service hatch set into one of the walls, and that's where we're heading.

"Some spy," I say, finding my voice again. "They won't need to see me coming – they can just arrest me while I'm lying there unconscious."

We stop at the hatch, and Helen smiles a greeting at the man standing behind it.

"Morning, Helen, what can I get you?" he asks.

"Hi Eric. Two coffees, please."

He nods and presses a button on a machine inside the kitchen, and a moment later hands through our cups. We claim a table and continue our conversation.

"Yeah, I heard you were having some issues."

"That's putting it mildly." I take a sip of my coffee and my lips curve into a pleasantly surprised smile –

Eric's machine makes a decent cup. "Yesterday I woke up in the middle of a field. I could ruin a lot of clothes getting the hang of this."

She nods.

"It was different for me; people started acting weirdly around me. It took me a long time to realise I was even doing anything."

"Scott says you can change people's perception of you." I can't quite work out how to word what I want to ask, but Helen gets where I'm going.

"That's not exactly it, though I suppose it's as good an explanation as any. It's difficult to explain. I can show you, if you want?"

"I'd like that."

"It can get pretty intense," she says, fixing me with a warning look. "What you felt yesterday was just a mild dose."

"I can handle it."

Or so I thought. But the sudden sensation running through me, it's… I feel like I've known Helen my entire life, like I could share my darkest secrets with her. In fact, I want to, no, I *need* to. I trust her so strongly that it's physically painful to think she might have an agenda, and the feeling of acceptance, it's so intense. Every other thought is washed from my mind. I close my eyes and bask in the sensation.

Suddenly it's gone. I open my eyes and freeze, staring in horror at the woman in front of me. Cold dread wells in my stomach and spreads through my veins, freezing me from the inside out. I feel the hairs on my arms stand up as the fear reaches my throat. My mouth pops open but no sound comes out, though I can feel my jaw working frantically. I leap back, knocking my chair over. I need to get away from her, I've got to get out of this place, I've got to–

A hand lands on my shoulder. I jump and spin around.

"Whoa, easy."

I blink several times, and Scott comes into focus. I drag a shaky breath into my lungs.

"What are you doing?" he snaps at Helen. "She doesn't have a handle on her talent yet – she could have shifted right out of here!"

"Relax," she says, apparently unperturbed. "She's tougher than you give her credit for."

"She was about to shift."

"I'm fine," I promise him. He stares at me for a moment, then nods and stoops to right my chair. I perch on it with a grateful smile and turn back to Helen.

"That was incredible!" The dread is completely gone.

"It has its uses."

With a sigh, Scott pulls out a chair and sits down.

"If you girls are done playing?"

"Sorry, Scott," Helen says, batting her eyelashes at him playfully. Scott rolls his eyes.

"Helen was just telling me about her talent," I say, reaching for my coffee cup. "I can't imagine having that level of control."

"It took a while," she says.

I pause, thinking about that. It's hard to imagine Helen losing control of anything. She always seems so composed.

"How long did it take?"

"Eighteen months, give or take. But then I didn't have access to any of this." She gestures to the room at large. "By the time Scott discovered me, I already had it well under control."

"Gave me quite the run-around, too," he adds.

She chuckles.

"The first time I met him, I thought he was a salesman."

"A salesman, in this suit," he says, plucking at his lapel.

"So I sent him running. It wasn't until he came back that I realised he was something else, and I used my little trick to get him to tell me everything."

I remember the compulsion I felt earlier and suppress a shudder – I was completely in Helen's thrall. It's easy to imagine why Scott was unable to resist.

"Yes, hilarious. You know Gardiner nearly demoted me over that, right?"

"Speaking of Gardiner…" Helen says, steering the conversation to more serious issues.

"Yeah, he wants to see you when you're done here."

Helen drains the dregs from her cup and rises.

"That's my cue. See you later, Anna."

"Bye, Helen."

"If you're done, we should probably get going too," Scott says as she leaves.

"Where are we going?" I ask, rising from my seat.

"Doctor Harwood is waiting to see you."

"Another doctor?" I ask, raising my eyebrows and feeling my enthusiasm drain. "How can there possibly be any tests left to run?"

"Doctor Harwood is a psychiatrist," Scott clarifies with a smile. I baulk and my feet stop moving of their own accord. Scott makes it a few more steps before he realises I'm not with him, but seems relieved to see me behind him – presumably he's pleased I haven't shifted, though that's only because I don't have enough control yet. Otherwise, I'd be long gone.

"A psychiatrist?" I manage to croak.

"It's just routine," he assures me. "There's nothing to worry about."

Nothing to worry about now, I consider pointing out. It might be a different story by the time they've finished poking around inside my head. Instead I sigh, and acknowledge that I don't really have a good enough excuse to get out of it. Normal people don't lose it about things like routine psych assessments.

"Fine, let's go," I grumble unwillingly, and shuffle along beside him. He's watching me closely as we ride in the lift – probably worried I'm going to shift again. I bite my lip and watch him back. Maybe I should give him a little more credit. He's watching me from the corner of his eye as he leans against the back of the lift, his expression innocent of any duplicitous intentions – he really does just seem concerned about me. And I know I've given him a hard time over the last couple of days. Any normal person would want shot of me and my erratic moods, but his face is still calm and patient. I'm not normally like this, a jumbled mess of anxiety and paranoia, but Scott has no way of knowing that. He's been more than fair with me, and he deserves better than I've been behaving.

With another sigh (and a mental note that I've been sighing much more than I used to over the last couple of days) I push myself off the side of the lift, but can't quite meet his eye.

"Sorry," I offer meekly. "I'm being an idiot."

"Listen to me, Anna," he says, lifting my chin lightly with one finger so I meet his eyes. "You have nothing to apologise for. I know how much of a big deal this is for you, and I'm glad you trust me enough to tell me when you're worried. But I promise, I'm not going to let anything happen to you."

I stare into his sincere blue eyes for a long second and feel him searching mine in return. I can feel the heat of his body, so close he's almost pressed against me, and make out the barest hint of the muscle beneath his shirt. I can taste the heady mix of his earthy scent and his cologne in the few inches between us. We both become aware of the electricity of his touch at the same moment and break apart awkwardly. He clears his throat.

"Sorry, that was completely inappropriate."

"No, I–" The lift jolts to a stop and the door slides back, cutting me off before I can formulate an end to the sentence. I'm glad for the excuse to look away from his eyes, not wanting to admit that my heart is racing, and for the first time in a long time, it's not from fear. I step out of the lift past the two suits waiting to enter, hoping they don't notice the flush of my cheeks, and I hear Scott step out behind me. He walks beside me along the corridor, but he's keeping a careful distance now. Great. Now I have to get through a psych assessment with my hormones all over the place like a damned teenager, and while I'm worrying about if things are going to be awkward between us. As if it wasn't going to be hard enough to start with.

I know, I know, at twenty-one I should be *way* better at this stuff. But the truth is, we moved around so much when I was a kid that I never stuck about in one place long enough to get attached to anyone, or have a proper relationship. Then I moved out and got my own place, and it's not like I've had a whole lot of time for guys since then, either, what with work and trying not to get evicted. Or a clue how to do anything about it if I do have an interest in a guy, beyond awkward smiles and close encounters in lifts. Guess my childhood really did screw me up. But for the love of God, don't tell Harwood that.

"This is it," Scott eventually says, breaking the silence. We've stopped outside a plain wooden door with a simple brass plaque screwed into it, bearing the name *Doctor Harwood*. I want to say something to Scott about what happened in the lift to dispel the weirdness, but thanks to my amazing social skills, I'm not quite sure what. He raises his hand and taps lightly on the door before I have time to organise my thoughts.

"Come in," a voice invites from inside.

"I'll be back by the time you're done," Scott promises, and then heads off down the hall. I watch his retreating back for a moment, then sigh and try to put him out of my mind. Plenty of time to worry about that disaster later. Timidly, I reach for the brass handle and ease the door open. The office is small and functional. Several bookcases line the walls, perched atop a thick burgundy carpet. There are two armchairs angled towards each other beside one wall, the leather creased with use, but not worn. They look comfortable and inviting, as does the brown fabric sofa pressed up against another wall. In common with the rest of the rooms I've seen inside AbGen, there are no windows, but the room is well lit and the atmosphere subtly relaxing. A small desk is set in one corner, organised and spartan, with just a laptop, a few sheaves of paper and a pen atop it. My eyes finally rest on the lady sitting behind it, wearing a simple dark skirt suit and elegant blouse. She's mid-thirties, with shoulder length dark hair, a pretty face, and an open expression. In short, she's not what I expected, although I suppose I should be past making assumptions about anything to do with AbGen by now – nothing here is what it seems. If ever there was a lesson about not judging a book by its cover…

"You must be Miss Mason," she says, stepping out from behind the desk and offering me her hand.

"Call me Anna." I accept her outstretched hand and offer her a smile. Her handshake is warm and firm, without the competitive edge some women get when attempting to prove themselves in a masculine environment. Doctor Harwood is clearly a woman confident in her status, without feeling the need to compete or intimidate.

"In that case, call me Sandra." She answers my smile with one of her own and then gestures to the two armchairs. "Please, take a seat."

I sink into one of the chairs – they're every bit as comfortable as they look – and sit awkwardly, watching her as she collects a notepad and pen from her desk drawer and relaxes into the chair opposite me.

By contrast, I'm sitting ramrod straight and I force myself to settle back into the soft leather. I cross my legs and entwine my fingers, twisting them in my lap, then catch myself in the act and stop, leaving one hand resting inside the other. With an uncomfortable cough, I uncross my legs, then press my knees together and hook one ankle over the other. When I look up, Sandra's watching me with an amused smile on her face.

"Try not to worry," she says, opening her notepad. "Think of this as an informal chat."

That's easy for her to say; she's not the one being analysed. Even so, I try to force an unconcerned expression as I wait for the interrogation to begin.

Chapter Nine

O kay, Anna," the white-coated man in front of me says with a nod, looking up from his clipboard. "Whenever you're ready."

Three pairs of eyes are watching me expectantly, and my gaze switches uneasily between them before looking round the room to distract myself from the growing knot in my gut. We're in one of the side rooms that branches off from the main lab, and beyond the door I can hear the muted buzz of AbGen's scientists at work, competing with the hum of machinery. There's another lab technician monitoring the computer, and a doctor whose job is apparently to monitor me – or my vital signs, at least. One of the scientists clears his throat, and I cast a glance over my shoulder to where Scott is towering protectively over my chair, reassuring myself of his presence. He smiles his encouragement and gives my shoulder a brief squeeze.

"Just relax, Anna. You can do this."

He sounds a lot more confident than I feel, and as my eyes pivot back to the two scientists and the doctor in front of me, I can see they're as dubious as I am. The lab technician taps briefly at the computer keyboard, and I see a flashing green dot appear on the screen, which represents me. Aside from relaying my location, the tracking device around my wrist is also measuring my heart rate and body temperature. The idea is that the doc and the lab techs will be able to monitor my physiological changes in real time, which they assure me is absolutely essential for some reason I don't quite follow. More importantly, to me at least, is that the tracking device will help them find me while I'm lying unconscious in whichever wet field or back alley my erratic talent dumps me in – preferably before I get mugged, raped or murdered, or all of the above.

The trouble is, I've never shifted intentionally before and the whole environment is way too clinical, and all the expectant pairs of eyes aren't exactly helping. I'm having a hard time focussing on anything besides the feeling that I'm right back in high school, standing centre stage and forgetting my lines. A voice in my head helpfully points out the irony that the one time I actually want to disappear, my body doesn't seem inclined to comply.

Shut up, I tell the voice, and tune out everything other than my breathing. I force it to come faster, taking shallower gasps of air and imitating my body's physical response to fear. I try to summon the feeling of dread that overwhelmed me right before I shifted accidentally every time over the last few days. My stomach twists half-heartedly in response, and the rest of my body is unconvinced. With a sigh, I give up and offer the perplexed-looking white coats a meek shrug.

I sense the movement behind me before I hear the rustle of clothing, and suddenly an arm is wrapped around my throat, pulling me tightly against the chair. I try to ask Scott what he's doing – this has got to be some sort of stupid joke, right? – but his arm is pressing on my windpipe and I can't get enough air. My mind scrambles to catch up as he leans down beside my ear, keeping the pressure on my neck.

"I knew we were wasting our time," he murmurs, his breath hot against my cheek.

"Do it," he orders the waiting scientists, who look startled but not worried by this turn of events. And that's when I realise. They're not the good guys. Not even close. I was such an idiot for trusting them. *Stupid, stupid, stupid!*

The chair in front of the monitor turns around, rotating towards me in slow motion. My lungs are burning, sending waves of panic through me and breaking me from my frozen immobility. I shruggle against my captor's arms, but he's too strong. There's no give in his grip or the chair, and the white coats are advancing on me. I thrash with everything I've got, twisting and squirming and grabbing at his arms like a drowning woman, but I'm no match for his strength and we both know it. But I can't give in, I've got to keep fighting, I've got to get out of here, I–

*

When I come round, the first thing I am aware of is that I'm lying on my side on a distinctly uncomfortable – and cold – surface, and the second is that the pounding in my head is back, but I don't think it's as bad as last time. I'm pretty sure that's going to change the moment I open my eyes.

"Anna, can you hear me?"

I groan and face the inevitable, forcing my lids apart, then freeze as the events in the lab come rushing back. My eyes flick to Scott's face from my prone position, and my hand flies to my throat. I scramble backwards and my back presses up against something solid and unyielding. My hands gropes behind me – a wall – but my eyes don't leave his face, waiting for him to continue his attack.

He doesn't. Instead, he's still crouching beside the spot in which I'd awoken, watching me calmly. My heart rate slows and I feel a red flush spread across my cheeks as I realise my own stupidity.

"You tricked me," I accuse, my eyes narrowing.

"Sorry," he apologises as he rises to his feet, but his tone isn't particularly repentant, nor does the smile tugging at the corner of his lips make it sound any more sincere.

"I'm glad you think it's funny," I snap, although my anger is somewhat undermined by the way my voice is shaking.

Scott's face is abruptly remorseful as he studies mine.

"I really am sorry," he says, offering me his hand. "I wish there was another way. I hate making you more afraid than you already are."

Yeah, me too. I'm not sure I like his way of 'helping'. But I guess his intentions were good, even if his method sucked. And it's not like there are any other shady government organisations offering to help me out. After a moment, I reach out and take his hand, letting him help me to my feet.

We're standing behind a block of flats, and I can tell we're not in a nice part of town because most of the windows are boarded up and the aging walls are lined with equally aging graffiti. The concrete beneath my feet is cracked and uneven, and stained with something that's giving off a distinctly unpleasant odour.

"Yeah, she's awake." I look up from the stains to see Scott talking into his phone. "We're heading back in."

I gather my wits as he puts the phone away, and ask,

"How long was I out for?"

"Thirty-eight minutes."

"You've been standing over my unconscious body for half an hour and no one called the cops?"

116

"Actually, I've only been here for ten minutes," he admits. "It took a little while to find you."

I suppose that's reasonable, not that it makes me feel any better about lying unconscious – unprotected – in an area where people clearly don't care what's happening to a passing stranger.

"What if I never stop passing out?" I groan. He opens his mouth, no doubt to reassure me, and I frown as his word choice finally hits home.

"What do you mean, 'to find me'?" I ask. Not reach me, find me.

He shuffles his feet and looks uncomfortable, taking a moment to meet my eye.

"When you shifted, all the machinery on our floor shut down. It took a while to get it back online. The tech guys think you gave off some sort of electro-magnetic pulse."

"Oh," is all I can think of to say. How odd. Although I suppose it explains why my disappearing act in front of several CCTV cameras in the shopping centre didn't make national news.

"You're very calm about this," he says. He's eyeing me suspiciously, and it occurs to me that I should probably be freaking out. I guess my mind is numb from all the shocks of the last few days, or I'm just beyond being surprised about anything now. Or maybe it's going to catch up with me when I think about the implications – like how my talent isn't just defensive anymore. Now, it's a weapon.

"Let's get you back to the car," he suggests, presumably having seen the blood drain from my face. I nod mutely and let him steer me back to the waiting vehicle.

It turns out I didn't travel very far, and we're back at AbGen less than ten minutes later.

"Why don't you head down to the canteen and get something to eat after you've seen Doctor Harwood?" Scott suggests as we pass through security. I guess I must still be a little pale. "I've got to run this to the med lab and then I'll join you."

I peer at the small vial he has produced, filled with red liquid, and then look down at my arm, noticing the tiny red scab there for the first time.

"When did you take that?" It probably shouldn't bother me as much as it does – I mean, at least I didn't have to watch him taking it.

"While you were out. The doc wants samples from after you shift so he can compare it to your normal bloodwork. He thinks it might help work out how you can control it better."

I sigh, resigned. It's really the least of my worries right now. And if I'm being honest, it's a small price to pay if it helps me get a handle on this crazy talent. I step out of the lift and trudge along the hallway with poor grace, trying not to think about what awaits me on the other side of Sandra's door. My first session was gruelling enough to make me feel anxious about my return visit, but apparently I'm going to have to accept the sessions as part of my regular schedule for as long as I'm at AbGen. It's as if they think that being part of an underground government organisation and being sent on secret missions might make me unstable. Wonder what gave them that idea?

I wait to be invited into the innocuous office, and perch on one of the too-comfortable armchairs.

"Good afternoon, Anna. How are you feeling?" she asks from behind her desk.

"Like I've been hit by a steamroller," I grumble in reply. "Do we really have to do this now?"

"It's vital I assess your state of mind as soon as possible after you use your talent if I'm to help you get control of it."

I drop my chin into my hands and she adds more sympathetically, "I'll keep it as short as possible. Can I get you a drink?"

"Coffee would be good."

"I… don't think that would be beneficial," she replies, rising from her seat. She lifts a teapot from a tray on a corner table I hadn't noticed before, and pours some of the steaming liquid into a mug. She splashes in a generous amount of milk and two sugars. It doesn't surprise me that she knows how I take my tea – Sandra is nothing if not thorough.

She hands me the mug and I blow softly on it, my breath displacing the steam from the surface. I take a sip and suddenly realise just how thirsty I am. I take another sip and enjoy the warming sensation as it hits my system. When I look up again, Sandra has settled into a chair opposite me with her notepad open and pen poised. I guess that means it's time to get down to business.

"So, this was your first attempt at shifting at will. I understand you had some... difficulties."

"I tried to get scared, like you said, but nothing happened."

"And why do you think that might be?"

I resist the urge to shrug, and give her question the consideration it deserves.

"My body wasn't buying it. I wasn't really afraid, not until Scott grabbed me..."

"Yes, you were able to shift quite quickly after that, weren't you?"

I nod and drain the rest of the cooling liquid from the mug. I'm already feeling better and starting to think more clearly.

"It strikes me that there are two possible reasons that you're not able to use your ability at will. The first is that you're incorrect about fear being the trigger." I'm already shaking my head; if there's one thing I can be certain of it's that I've been terrified every time right before I shifted, but she ignores me and continues, "And the second is that in a lab scenario you're more afraid of the consequences of using your ability than you are of the stimulus."

I take a moment to process that. She might not be far wrong – she knows how I feel about trusting authority figures, and you don't get more vulnerable than showing your mutant power to a bunch of people who'd like to get a good look inside your brain. She knows I'd wish this damned talent away if I could, too.

"Let's talk about how you felt right after you shifted."

Despite all of Sandra's promises about keeping it short, it's over an hour later when she finally lets me leave. I head straight to the canteen, but a quick glance around tells me I've beaten Scott here. That's odd. I wonder what's kept him. Panic flutters in my stomach. Has something weird shown up in my blood? I push the thought aside and make an effort to silence my overactive imagination.

"Two coffees please, Eric," I say as I reach the service hatch. I'm sure Scott won't be far behind me. I run my eye over the chalkboard menu while we wait for the machine and try to decide whether any of it is likely to be edible, and also whether my stomach is likely to be able to hold any of it down. The chicken soup looks like it's probably a safe option, so I ask Eric for a bowl and he promises to bring it over.

The canteen is mostly deserted – a quick glance at the clock tells me I've missed the lunchtime rush – so I claim a table in the corner where I can see the door and settle down to wait for Scott. I dedicate a bit of time to idle daydreaming, marvelling at how much my life has changed since he came barging into it. I'm glad the awkwardness from our non-event in the lift didn't linger. My mind runs back over his tender contact, and I can't help wondering what would have happened if I'd had the guts to say what I was really thinking; if I'd raised my hand and touched his face, drawn him towards me and–

A tray clatters onto the table in front of me, shattering my fantasy. I look up guiltily into Eric's apologetic face.

"Sorry, Anna. Say, are you okay? You look a little pale."

"I'm fine, thanks, Eric. You just made me jump," I lie. He apologises again and then disappears, leaving me alone with the steaming soup and my steamy thoughts. I chastise myself for the errant daydream – I've forbidden myself from thinking about Scott in that way. You'd think him almost throttling me this morning would have driven that particular fantasy from my mind, but apparently not. I dip the spoon into the thick liquid, pausing to blow on it, and then take a tentative sip. I'm pleasantly surprised – the soup is definitely edible, and I can't help but wonder if Eric poured it out of a tin. He doesn't seem a likely chef.

My stomach churns in reaction to the warm food, but as I take another mouthful, then another, I start to feel better. I'm over halfway through by the time Scott appears and takes a seat in front of his tepid coffee. He takes a sip and grimaces, then sets it aside. I watch him closely for a moment, startled to realise that he looks even more exhausted than I am. I hope he's not losing sleep over the trouble I'm causing. I would comment on it, but I'm feeling way too awkward after catching myself thinking about him in a very non-professional capacity. I lower my spoon into my soup to mask my embarrassment, but I've lost my appetite. Deprived of my distraction, I abandon the spoon and look up to catch him staring at me intently.

"Do I have soup on my face?" I ask him, and feel myself turning red. I'm such a messy eater. I look for a napkin on the tray and realise there isn't one.

"Sou–? No," he says, appearing embarrassed himself, like I'd caught him spying on an intimate moment.

"Oh." I look back down at my soup, then push it aside. "So, what's the plan for this afternoon?"

Scott pounces on the change of topic.

"The techs have prepared a new lab for us, if you feel up to making another attempt?"

"Sure, why not?"

He's still scrutinising my face, and I wonder what he's seeing there – fear? Reluctance, frustration? Or anticipation? I'm more enthusiastic about the training session than I'd expected. So much for wishing my talent away. That brings me back to Sandra's theories. I outline them briefly for Scott, who looks thoughtful for a moment. He'd better not be planning any more tricks.

"Ready?" he asks.

"Let's do it."

I'm soon back sitting in the same chair as this morning, but everything else has changed. Only one of the white coats from earlier is here, the one with shaggy, unkempt hair and glasses – Toby, I think his name is – and he has the decency to look a little sheepish. Apparently the other two are monitoring us from another room, which is just as well since this one is tiny. Even with just the three of us, it's more than a little cramped in here. The walls are lined with some sort of plating, which will apparently stop my EM pulse from disrupting anything outside of this room. Part of me is impressed that Gardiner hasn't ordered them to see how strong the pulse is in order to weaponise it. The other part of me wonders if he's just waiting until I have some control over it.

The white coat is nodding; either in response to a gesture from Scott or a voice in his earpiece, I'm not sure which.

"Okay, Anna, when you're ready."

I have nothing to fear from shifting, I remind myself, trying to get comfortable in a chair that clearly wasn't designed for comfort. I've can trust these guys. If Sandra's theory is right, then I just need to work through it. The headache and nausea will pass. Okay, so I'm not exactly thrilled about the blackouts, but the more I shift, the sooner Doc Maynard can work out what's causing them and fix it. Scott will be there by the time I wake up. And, honestly, the whole thing scares me a whole lot less now that I know I'm not losing my mind.

I exhale slowly and close my eyes, and focus on the terror I felt back in the shopping centre when I was stealing that stupid ring. I bring it to the centre of my mind: the stones on the ring's surface biting into the palm of my hand, the shocked gasps and startled stares of the other shoppers, the desperate need to escape. The fear has imprinted the scene in my memory and it's like I'm living it again: I can hear the sound of boots on metal ringing in my ears, signalling the proximity of my pursuers, but I don't dare to look at how close they are.

I reach the bottom step and get ready to run again. Something snags my shirt. A hand. I twist and manage to wrench myself free, but as I look across the empty floor to the exit, the second cop appears and cuts me off. I skid to a halt, swivelling my head around frantically. How did he get in front of me? I don't have time to think about it – I have to find a way out. I can't go forward, I can't go back, and I can't let them catch me. I've only got a split second to react, to do something, anything – I've got to get out of here, I've got to–

Chapter Ten

Aweek has passed since I first shifted at will, and it gets easier with every attempt. The blackouts and headaches are still a feature, but the nausea is thankfully a thing of the past. The white coats theorise that my body has simply gotten used to the sensation of shifting. Apparently, they have a theory about the headaches and blackouts as well, which they're keen to 'discuss' with me this morning. I'm headed there now, on my shiny new motorcycle, courtesy of AbGen (since, although I can shift at will, I still can't control where I end up, so it's not really practical for commuting.) I turned down their offer of a flat closer to Langford House, partly because the idea of them having that much control of my life creeps me out, and partly through a desire to cling to something familiar in all of this craziness.

I quit my job at the restaurant, of course – though it was hard not being able to tell them what I was really doing. I gave them the thin cover story concocted by Scott, which Lloyd had swallowed whilst muttering about having to find a replacement at short notice, but Janey eyed me suspiciously, hugged me fiercely and told me not to be a stranger – a promise there's no way I can keep. Leading a secret life and having girly nights out just aren't compatible, and keeping my secret has to take priority. Plus, who knows what shady world I'm getting involved in? It would be unforgivable to put Janey at risk for my own selfish reasons. I miss her like crazy, but AbGen have got me on such a hectic schedule that I haven't had much time to feel lonely.

Despite Scott's best efforts, my feelings towards Gardiner haven't warmed. Scott doesn't get it, given everything the man has done for me, but it's not something I can explain. I just don't trust him. Every time I think of him, I see the look on his face the first day we met. I guess it's true what they say: first impressions count. I try to keep him from my thoughts and focus on the positives instead, like my gorgeous new motorbike. No speeding tickets so far, which is another positive.

I pull into AbGen's car park and leave my bike next to Scott's, then make my way through security into Langford House. The armed guard who had terrified me only a couple of weeks ago now seems like part of the scenery: I barely bat an eyelid other than to nod a greeting. His name's Joe and he's actually a nice guy, once you get past the gun and the creepy tattoo. It turns out he got it as a dare during his military days. He's not much older than me, but he has a wife at home who gave birth to a boy a couple of months ago. Joe carries photos of mother and baby in his wallet, which he proudly shows to anyone who asks. I find it hard to believe that Mrs Joe is entirely okay with his career choice, but that said, I understand that AbGen's generosity extends to all of its employees, and this has got to be a whole lot safer than being deployed in the Middle East. And it can't hurt, what with Joe being a mind reader, which I imagine must come in handy for sensing when visitors have an ulterior motive. It takes a lot of focus apparently, and homing in on a specific person's thoughts leaves him drained, but still.... way cooler than erratic shifting.

I check in with Nora behind her bullet-proof glass – Nora, of course, is his handler, I don't know how I didn't spot it before – and then duck into the lift, heading up to the rec room to lose my helmet and leathers. When I step through the doors, Scott is already waiting for me. I spare a quick glance at the clock on the wall: nope, not late. He's obviously angling for employee of the month.

"Morning, Anna," he says, with a genuine smile.

"Morning," I return the greeting, stripping off my leathers and carefully placing my helmet inside my locker. "So, what's on the agenda for today?"

"Another exciting day of physical training," he says with entirely too much mirth – he knows how I feel about working out. "But first things first – we need to get you down to the lab before the techs explode with excitement about their latest idea."

"That good, huh?" I ask with a raised eyebrow, because truth be told I have a hard time visualising the lab guys getting excited about anything except superhero movies.

A few minutes later, we push through the doors into the lab. Toby practically leaps from his seat when he sees us; Scott wasn't exaggerating about how excited he is about this revelation of his. Two more white coats join us, though I notice Doctor Pearce isn't here – apparently he's not so excited about this discovery.

"Hi, Toby."

"Hey Anna," he says, and then a quarter second later: "What's the one thing you've wanted since the day you got to AbGen?"

"You mean you've built me a jet-pack?" I gush with mock enthusiasm.

Toby's face falls momentarily.

"Uh– I could probably build you a jet-pack," he rushes with a nervous swallow, pushing his glasses up his nose. "I mean, it can't be that hard, you'd need to give me a few days, but I think I–"

"Anna…" Scott says reproachfully, shooting me a disapproving look.

"I'm sorry, Toby." It's easy to forget that these guys don't get out of the lab much. "I was only joking. You know the only thing I want is to be rid of these blackouts."

"In that case, I'm your man," he says, his face lighting up again.

"Seriously? You've found a way to stop them?"

One of the white coats behind Toby elbows him, and he amends his statement.

"We *might* have found a way. But we need to run a few tests first."

"I'm game," I say, with a quick glance at Scott to make sure I've got time before the PT session from hell – scheduling never was my strong suit. He doesn't raise any objections.

"Okay then, this way please, m'lady," Toby says, gallantly sweeping his arm in the direction of the EM shielded room. I lift the hem of an imaginary dress and curtsey, then lead the five of us into the tiny room.

"Tadaa!" he announces, producing an innocuous-looking white pill.

"Uh, I'm pretty sure there are rules about taking magic pills at work."

"Ha ha." This time apparently my sense of humour isn't wasted on him. "But seriously, Anna, this might be the answer you've been looking for. How much do you know about how your ability works?"

"I get scared, panic, and wake up some place else with a headache."

"Well, yes, that's true," he says, "but biologically speaking, it's a little more complex than that. When your body gets ready to shift, it dumps an enormous amount of epinephrine – adrenaline – into your system, which in turn burns through your body's glucose reserves in order to generate the EM pulse and shift. We're not sure if the EM pulse is a side effect of the shift, or vice versa, but either way it completely depletes your blood sugar levels and leaves you hypoglycaemic. The hypoglycaemia causes the blackout, and it's responsible for your headaches when you regain consciousness, which doesn't happen until your body compensates and your blood sugar levels start to climb again."

His explanation seems long winded and overly complex, and leaves a frown on my face as I attempt to decipher it. His face is lit up with excitement and he's practically bouncing on the balls of his feet as he waits for me to catch up.

"So, let me get this straight," I manage after a moment. "I just need more sugar?"

He nods, looking extremely proud of himself. He should be. That's about the best news I've heard all week.

"How does it work?"

"Okay, so this–" he gestures to the pill, "–is actually just a glucose pill. You chew it thoroughly and then wait ten minutes for it to get into your bloodstream. Elliot made this one. It's more potent than the over-the-counter varieties, so you should only need one."

Behind him, Elliot beams with pride at the acknowledgement. These guys are clearly starved of attention. I make a mental note to send them some chocolates.

"Now hopefully," Toby continues, apparently keen to get my attention back, "it means that your body's going to have enough glucose to help you shift, without draining your reserves and leaving you unconscious. It might take a little trial and error to get the dosage right, though."

Behind him, Elliot nods, and adds in his own warning.

"You should bear in mind that you don't want to take this more than half an hour before you're planning on shifting – otherwise your body will release insulin to cope with all the excess glucose, and you're going to end up worse off than you started."

"Okay then, let's do it," I say, and chew the pill. Elliot and the other technician spend the next ten minutes fussing around, getting me equipped with the tracker and making sure it's set up with the computer in the next room, while Toby checks his watch every few seconds.

When I'm certain I can't stand it a moment longer, he finally gives me the nod.

"Okay, that's ten minutes, and the computer's set. Whenever you're ready, Anna."

I nod and settle back in my chair, closing my eyes and allowing the feeling of terror to build, until I can't stand to be here, I've got to move, I've got to get out of here, I've got to–

I stagger, and reach my hand out to the wall – and that's when I realise I'm not in the lab any more, and neither am I on the floor unconscious.

"It worked," I gasp. It's official: Toby is a genius. I'm going to owe him more than chocolates for this one. I take a moment to get my breath and do a mental inventory. My head is pounding but it's bearable. The nausea is back, but mild compared to when I first shifted. I feel a little dizzy, but all things considered, if this is the trade-off for not blacking out, I'll take it.

I look around, glad as always that my erratic talent has dumped me somewhere away from prying eyes, although yet again I have no idea where I am. There's a lot of grey around me – smooth grey walls, grey asphalt floor, high spiked railings with the paint faded to expose bare metal. The only traces of colour are the weeds growing through the cracks. It looks like I'm outside an abandoned warehouse; a smashed window suggests that the only people who come out this way are kids. I pull out my phone to check in with Scott and see that it's still rebooting itself. Right, because of the EM pulse. That's going to get old. Luckily, the tracker around my wrist is shielded, so hopefully Scott is already on his way.

When the nausea fades to a tolerable level, I walk around the edge of the compound, looking for a way out. The flat spiked railings are so close together that I can't see what's beyond them: I squint through a gap but see only green foliage. After a few minutes I find the gate – at least, I assume it's the gate – a hole has been cut in the rails and a chain fed through it. I pull the chain, but something blocks its progress. I give it another yank but am rewarded with nothing more than a louder rattle. Another squint tells me it's a padlock, and it looks like it's securely locked. Not that it would matter anyway, since I can't get my hand through the gap to release it.

Just typical. What sort of stupid talent leaves me trapped inside a locked yard? If I had any sort of control over this, I could just shift back to Langford House and save all this messing around – but I guess that would actually be useful. With a stamp of my foot, I let go of the chain and stare up at the grey sky above me. Looks like I'm just going to have to sit here and wait to be rescued.

Sitting still doesn't work for me, so I pace around the courtyard some more, pondering why exactly it is that I can't control where I shift to. After all, the first time I shifted, I wound up back at my flat, and that was pretty specific. But since then, it's been completely unpredictable. The playing field, that alley two towns over, and a whole host of places since there. None of them have anything in common. But there has to be some way that my body is selecting these places – surely it can't just be completely random?

I pull my phone out of my pocket again, just to keep my hands busy – it's finally coming to life. The screen lights up and the signal bars reluctantly flash up. Immediately, it rings. The display flashes up Jaqen H'ghar, which is what I have Scott's number programmed as. I hit answer and take the call.

"Hey, Scott, what's up?"

"Anna, you're alright. Thank God." He covers the mouthpiece and speaks to someone, and I frown at the relief in his tone. It's not like him to get flustered.

"Yeah, I'm fine," I tell him, working to keep the confusion out of my voice and failing. I want to ask him why I wouldn't be, but I don't want to sound defensive, so I move to a more pressing issue. "How far away are you? It looks like rain." I glance down at my cotton t-shirt doubtfully and try to remember what the weather had been like when I pulled up at Langford House this morning. Scott doesn't answer my question.

"Scott?"

"Okay… don't panic, Anna – but you're in France."

Chapter Eleven

I stagger back against the wall, reaching my hand out for support. France… How… Why… France!

"Anna?" Scott's distant voice buzzes persistently in my ear until I can't ignore it anymore.

"Anna, can you hear me?"

It takes me a moment to find my voice, and when I do, it doesn't sound like my own.

"I'm here. I'm… not panicking." Oh no, I'm way beyond panicking. It's taking everything I've got just to hold myself in one place. Maybe that's why I sound so breathless.

"Just sit tight – try not to shift."

What does he think I'm doing??

"We're on our way, Anna, just stay calm."

Easier said than done, I think. Or maybe I said it out loud, because Scott is asking me,

"Remember that day down at the lake?"

The day I decided to accept AbGen's offer – how could I forget?

"You remember skimming stones, and the birds circling overhead?" he continues, his voice soothing and calm. "Just focus on the lake."

Birds circling above the lake, birds circling above the lake. I let the image fill my mind… their graceful outlines as they drifted through the thermals, the way the breeze blew ripples across the lake's surface, the sun glinting off the calm water. I take a few breaths and keep playing the image in my mind until the panicky thudding of my heart has subsided. As much as it's going to, anyway. I'm in France. Alright, it's not ideal, but it's not the end of the world.

"Okay, I'm good," I tell Scott with as much conviction as I can muster. "What now?"

"Tell me what you can see. The area you're in is showing up as a blank zone on the map."

"I'm inside some sort of compound, it looks like there's an abandoned warehouse." I try to peer through the railings again. "I can't see what's outside."

Someone speaks at the other end of the line, but the voice is too muffled to make out, and then Scott curses loudly, and I hear the vehicle's engine scream as someone floors the accelerator.

"What?" I ask, a note of alarm returning to my voice.

"Nate thinks you might be in a French special forces training site – that's why nothing's showing up on the map."

"And what happens if they find me here?"

"It's probably best you get out of there before that happens."

"Uh, slight problem with that," I tell him. "The gate's locked and the fences are too high to climb."

"Okay, don't panic," he says, but his voice is too urgent to be comforting. He seems to realise, and moderates his tone. "Just try to lie low. If you get caught, don't resist."

"I could shift," I say. Not panicking be damned. I need to get the hell out of here. "Anywhere's got to be–"

"No," he cuts across me. "You might not make it far so soon after your last shift, and at least right now you're conscious."

An image of myself, passed out, defenceless, lying in the path of the French forces flashes through my mind and I suppress a shudder.

"Don't shift. Got it. Scott..."

"I know," he says, and I can hear the firm set of his lips in his voice. "We're coming as fast as we can."

I shuffle along to the broken window and raise myself up on my tiptoes. I can't make out much in the gloom, but inside looks spacious and deserted – and much less exposed than standing out here waiting to be caught.

"There's a broken window," I tell Scott. "I think I can get inside. Should I try?"

The muffled voices start again. I pick out Scott's amongst them and strain to hear what he's saying, but it's like listening to an untuned radio – the odd words I can make out make no sense. Then I make out the word "captured" in Nathan's voice, and my stomach lurches. I stop trying so hard to listen.

After what seems like an age, Scott comes back on the line.

"It's too risky. Nate thinks if you get caught, it's going to look a lot more suspicious if you're inside than if you're outside. I agree."

"I can't just stand here waiting to be spotted."

"I know. Is there anywhere you can hide?"

I scan the area, looking for anything tall enough to hide behind, or big enough to hide inside. I spot a concrete tunnel – the sort they use for laying underground drains – and jog over to take a closer look. It's about seven feet in length and a couple of feet wide.

"Anna?"

"There's a concrete tunnel, like a drainage pipe – I think I can fit inside it."

"Okay, good. But first you need to get rid of the tracker – the technology is years ahead of anything available to the public. You'll never be able to explain it away. Chuck it over the fence – if you get taken, we'll have you out before anyone can find it."

Taken. Shit. I tug the tracker from my wrist and throw it up at the fence. My hands are shaking and it falls short, bouncing off the railings and clattering to the ground. I scoop it up in trembling fingers, take a breath and hurl it as high as I can over the fence. I hear a muted thud as it falls through the foliage on the other side and hits the sodden mud, then make my way back to the concrete tube.

I drop to my hands and knees, keeping the phone pressed to my ear with one hand, and crawl inside. It's tight, but if I can just twist – there – I can sort of sit and look outside, albeit from an awkward position.

"Good. Now, what's my number programmed into your phone as?"

I tell him, and hear a humourless chuckle from Nathan.

"Change it to DS Yates – I'll stay on the line."

I pull the phone away from my ear and make the change, remembering his fake police credentials the day I found him inside my flat. I can't help feeling they won't hold much sway with the French Special Forces.

"If anyone asks, you're a witness in a murder case – you've changed your mind about running and want to come in."

He carries on fleshing out my cover story – I try to absorb as much as I can – in between reassuring me that this is just a precaution and that it's unlikely anyone will come out here.

I interrupt him in a hoarse whisper that sounds too loud inside the tunnel.

"I can hear someone coming. They're opening the gate."

"Okay, now listen to me very carefully, Anna. If they sweep the compound, they're going to find you. You need to do *exactly* what they say."

"I don't speak any French," I confess.

"At all?"

"No, I took German."

"Dammit. Okay, this is what you're going to do. When they find you, crawl out of the tunnel – slowly. Put your hands on your head and say '*Je ne parle pas français*'. Do you understand?"

"Mm-hmm," I answer, as quietly as I can. The compound is filling up with a dozen men, each one carrying a gun.

"We're an hour away, Anna, you've just got to hang in there. And whatever you do, you can't let them see you shift."

"*Sortez avec vos mains vers le haut!*"

The command must have travelled along the line, because Scott says,

"You need to crawl out now, Anna."

"*Sortez avec vos mains vers le haut!*" The command comes again, louder this time. The soldiers have fanned out into a semi-circle around my tunnel, and all of them are pointing their vicious-looking weapons at me.

"Go! And Anna... I– We're coming."

I pull the phone away from my ear with shaking hands and stuff it into my pocket. Slowly, I crawl forward, and as soon as my head is poking out I raise my hands, and shuffle out on my knees. A soldier in the centre of the semi-circle barks another instruction, which I assume means stop. I do, and kneel there with my hands behind my head while the soldiers advance, weapons still raised.

"*Je ne parle pas français*," I tell the one who spoke to me, then look frantically around the advancing faces. "Please don't hurt me."

"Sur le sol!" the soldier barks at me.

"*Je ne parle pas français*," I insist.

He exchanges a look with another soldier, and gives a curt nod.

"On the floor," the other soldier instructs in heavily accented English, and my head snaps to him. "Face down."

Relieved that I'm not about to be shot for skipping high school French, I lower myself onto my stomach. But my relief is premature.

"Hands behind your head," the same voice snaps. "Interlock your fingers."

I do as he says, and try to get a look at them from my new perspective. All I can see are several pairs of boots and a pair of kneecaps. None of them seem to be moving, and I'm not sure if that's a good thing or a bad thing. Somehow, I doubt they're going to let me lie here until Scott comes to rescue me.

"Eyes down."

With an effort, I force my gaze back down onto the ground in front of me, against every instinct in my body screaming at me not to take my eyes off them – for all the difference it would make.

"Please don't hurt me," I plead again into the asphalt.

"*Taisez-vous!*"

I can't see who said it, but I assume it was an instruction to shut up, so I do. A pair of boots move to stand a little in front of me, and I can practically feel the weapon pointing at me. I can hear another pair of boots moving to my side, but bite down on my lip and force myself to keep looking away. My ears are straining to pick up any sound that might give a clue what he's planning, but I can barely hear a thing above the beating of my own heart. Something touches my shoulder and I flinch, then steady myself. It's a hand, I realise, as a second one joins it on my other shoulder. I keep very still as the soldier pats me down, his rough hands fast and business-like. He pauses at my pocket and pulls out my phone and a couple of coins. I mutter a silent prayer of thanks that AbGen insist we don't carry anything that can identify ourselves – I'd thought it was silly at the time. I don't now.

The hands carry on searching, but there's nothing left to find. He grabs one of my wrists and I flinch again. He pulls it behind my back and brings the other to join it, then binds them together using what I think might be a plasticuff – I can feel the edges digging into my skin. A sack is pulled over my head, and suddenly I'm surrounded by darkness and the sound of my breathing. Panic wells in my stomach again, and the adrenaline coursing through my body threatens to make me shift. I take a long moment to calm myself, and to remind myself that Scott is coming, and that they're just doing this to intimidate me. It's working.

Two pairs of arms seize me and pull me roughly to my feet. Still holding my arms, they start walking, and I stumble along between them. It's completely disorientating with the sack over my face, and several times I trip and nearly fall, but the hands hold me up.

"Where are you taking me?" I ask desperately into the black. The only answer I get is the heat and moisture of my breath reflecting back off the inside of the hood. One of the hands jerks me to a halt, and I stand still, straining my ears for any clue as to where we are, or where we might be going. Another set of hands reaches down and hauls me upwards. I try not to resist, but every part of me tenses as my feet leave the ground. Terror sends a flash of heat through me. My feet finally find some purchase and I scramble backwards, assisted by the hands.

"Lie down," a voice barks, and I do so awkwardly, struggling without the use of my hands and my eyesight to guide me. The floor is cold and metallic, and the voice echoes around me – maybe some sort of van. A few seconds later, it roars into life, confirming my suspicion. It's not until the vehicle starts to rumble along the track that the reality of my situation really hits me. I'm bound and blindfolded in the back of a van, surrounded by strangers who clearly don't harbour any good intentions towards me, heading off to somewhere Scott might not be able to find me, especially with my tracker lying in a ditch. What the hell am I doing? I need to get away! I've got to get out of here, I've got to– No! I've got to… stay. Got… to wait… for… Scott…

Chapter Twelve

I awaken and open my eyes, but the darkness is absolute. Why is it so dark, why can't I see? I can feel the heat and moisture of my breath crowding me claustrophobically, feel something clinging to my mouth as I gasp the stagnant air. The hood. It's just the hood.

Oh shit. The French military. The realisation hits me like a fist to the gut. Scott warned me – I've revealed my secret. I just shifted in front of a van full of French soldiers – there's no way we can cover this up! I make myself take a deep, slow breath, and then another. Panicking isn't going to help. *Nothing* is going to help. I'm screwed. But right now I can't worry about that. I have to work out where I am, and find somewhere to hide.

My hands are going numb from the plasticuffs, and my shoulders are burning from being pulled up behind my back. I wriggle my fingers and try to get some feeling back into them. I need to get this damned hood off so I can work out where I am.

"*Ne bouge pas!*" a voice orders me.

I freeze. Where am I? Wait, am I still with the French forces? How is that possible – did they recapture me while I was out? The floor beneath me moves, almost sending me rolling to one side. I'm still in the vehicle. I'm not sure how I didn't notice sooner; we're travelling at speed and I can feel every bump in the road jolting through my spine. Could I have shifted and been recaptured? No. There's no way they could have found me that quickly, and if they had, I'm pretty sure they'd be treating me a lot differently by now.

Then I didn't shift. I must've passed out. Maybe my body hadn't recovered from the last shift enough to attempt a second. Whatever the reason, my secret's safe – which is more than I can say for me. I have no idea how long I was out for, or where we are.

As if in answer to my thoughts, the van stops and someone kills the engine. The sudden silence is oppressive, and then the doors swing open. Hands seize me from behind and pull me to my feet, dragging me out.

We must be in some sort of building, because I don't hear any wind rushing around me, or feel it on my exposed arms. I hear two voices and strain to catch what they're saying, but I can't quite make it out and it's probably in French, anyway. Resigned to being kept in the dark – figuratively and literally – I allow myself to be led forwards again, meekly obeying my captors. *How much longer until Scott gets here?*

We follow what must be a long corridor, taking countless twists and turns, and the further we go, the more disorientated I become, until I'm certain I would never find my way out of here alone. A hand jerks me roughly to a halt and I stand rigid, listening intently, but I can't hear anything above the blood pounding in my ears.

Fingers wrap around my wrist and I flinch away, but the grip only tightens and yanks me back into place. I bite back a sob and screw my eyes shut. *It'll be over soon, it'll be over soon, oh God, please let me get out of here soon.*

I feel the plasticuffs tugging at my wrists and biting into my skin. Something cold and hard brushes against my wrist, and instinctively I know it is a knife. My breath catches in my throat and I force myself to go very still. Abruptly it's gone and I feel the cuffs fall away, leaving my hands unbound. I fight the urge to rub my wrists as the blood rushes back into my hands, hyper aware of the fingers still digging into my forearm.

My right arm is pulled in front of me and pressed onto a surface at waist height. My exposed fingers curl themselves into a fist, trying to get away from whatever horrible thing is about to happen to them. My hand trembles and I shrink back, colliding with something – someone – behind me. He grabs the back of my t-shirt and pushes me forwards again, and the whole while my hand is pinned in place.

"Open your hand." I can't tell if it's just his accented English that makes him sound angry, but reluctantly I force my trembling fingers to stretch out. The surface

150

beneath them is smooth, like glass. The soldier takes my thumb and rolls the tip from one side to the other. They're fingerprinting me, I realise with a feeling akin to relief. Relief that's short-lived. Who knows what information they can get about me? I just have to trust that the guys at AbGen know their stuff. Truth be told, I'm running a little low in the trust department right now, so I think of happier thoughts. Scott is coming. Every second he's getting closer, and he's going to get me out of here. I cling to the comforting thought like a life raft as the rest of my prints are taken. My wrists are pulled behind me again and a pair of metal handcuffs ratchets shut.

Another hand closes around my arm and pulls me away. I lose my balance and stumble, but the iron grip keeps me upright, biting into my arm. Between the movement and the darkness, nausea hits me with overwhelming force. I retch into the hood, but the hand forces me onwards without mercy. I gulp in the stale air urgently. The darkness and the heat of my own breath are suddenly claustrophobic. Sweat prickles my forehead and I gasp frantically, the hood being pulled into my mouth with each breath. My feet have no choice but to keep moving at the soldier's pace, but my every instinct is screaming at me to run… or shift. No, I can't shift, Scott is coming. Scott is coming.

My breaths come a little easier and I try to focus on what's happening around me. A door creaks open in front of me and we walk through. A moment later, it shuts with a bang that echoes around the room.

"Sit."

My bound hands grope behind me and brush against something – a chair. Cautiously, I lower myself into it and the hand releases its grip on my arm. I hear boots crossing the floor and then the door opens and closes again. I think I'm alone. I listen intently and hear only my own breathing. I daren't attempt to remove the hood, and with my hands still cuffed behind my back, I'm not sure I could even if I wanted to.

I lean back in the chair, breathing deeply, and close my eyes. The darkness feels more natural that way, like I can fool myself into believing it's my choice. I know what's coming next, though, and my stomach knots at the thought of it. Sooner or later they will come for me, and if they think I'm a foreign spy, they're not going to hold anything back. It all hinges on them believing my cover story. I have to buy enough time for Scott to find me, or– I stop that thought before it can form. I need to focus.

My name is Gemma Hanson. Three weeks ago, I saw Ronnie Marsden, drug dealer and gang leader, kill his girlfriend. One of the cops investigating the case – DS Yates – has been trying to persuade me to give evidence.

Ronnie's gang has threatened to kill me if I do. Fear getting the better of me, last night I took off, with no plan in mind other than to get as far away from London as I could.

Personally, I think Gemma would have to be stupid to run to another country without a solid plan in mind, but Scott was adamant that most people in that situation would be more worried about what they were running from than what they were running to. I hope he's right, because it's the only cover story I've got.

I run the story through my mind over and over as I sit alone in the dark. They've taken my phone and I didn't have a watch to start with, so I have no way of knowing how much time passes. It feels like a long time, though. I try to remind myself that anything that buys me time is a good thing – I don't have to convince them to let me go, just that I'm not a foreign spy, and avoid being moved again for long enough to give Scott a chance to find me.

If my hands weren't bound behind my back, I'd have slumped my head into them. When am I going to get a handle on this stupid talent? The only time I seem to have had any sort of control over where I end up was before I even knew I could shift. I open my eyes and frown, thinking about that a moment. What was so different about that first shift, back when I stole the ring?

The answer is so obvious it stuns me. In the shopping centre, my overwhelming desire had been to get away, but it wasn't my only desire. I wanted to be in the only place I considered safe: home. It's so obvious that it's all I can do to remember where I am and keep myself from laughing. If I can just recreate that feeling, maybe I can control where I end up. It's like Scott said about Gemma: I've been so busy focussing on what I'm running from, trying to make myself shift, that I haven't put any thought into where I was running to.

Perhaps the cover story is more believable than I gave it credit for, then. Any lingering thoughts of laughter die instantly. It doesn't matter if I'm right about controlling where I go, because shifting is the one thing I can't risk right now.

A door slams loudly behind me and I jump, my nerves getting the better of me. Footsteps click across the floor and the hood is abruptly yanked from my head. I blink rapidly, my pupils contracting as they work frantically to adjust to the stark light. I look around. I'm inside a small room dominated by a table that's bolted to the wall and floor, with two chairs on either side of it. The walls are bare and have no windows, though it barely registers after all the time I've spent at AbGen. The soldier who removed my hood steps back to stand stoically by the door. It does not escape my notice that he is armed. I can't tell if he's one of the soldiers who captured me: I spent more time staring at their boots than their faces.

There's a second soldier in the room, and he's the one who holds my attention. Mid-forties, lean, and hard-faced, there's no mistaking his air of authority. I watch him warily from the corner of my eye as he positions himself in the seat opposite me, unable to make myself look directly at him. My breath catches in my throat and I swallow noisily. I've got to hold it together better than this or I'll never last until Scott finds me.

I force my eyes from the table top and see him watching me impassively.

"You are English," he says, his voice heavily accented. It is a statement, not a question. I answer anyway.

"Yes, sir," I say meekly. Scott had warned me to acknowledge their authority right from the off, but even without the warning, I'm way too terrified to give him any attitude.

"I am going to ask you who you are, and why you have come here."

I look him in the eye and prepare to lie.

He raises a hand. "Stop. Whatever lies you are about to tell me, think carefully. I will give you this one chance to tell me the truth. Do not squander it."

I quail beneath his fierce stare and avert my eyes. How much does he know? I'm hanging everything on the hope that AbGen got my cover story into the system in time. I don't want to find out what they'll do to me if they catch me lying. I bite back tears.

"I just want to go home."

"Tell me your name."

"Gemma Hanson."

Please let it match up with my fingerprints. He continues to stare at me in silence, and then nods to the soldier behind me. He approaches and takes hold of my wrists. I flinch, and then force myself to stay still. A moment later, the cuffs come away and the soldier returns to his post by the door.

"Good. I am glad you have decided to cooperate, Gemma."

I rub my wrists, trying to massage some feeling back into them, whilst steadfastly avoiding looking at my captor.

"I am Colonel Morel. If you are honest with me, things will go better for you. Lie, and I will not be able to help you."

I nod my understanding.

"You are in a lot of trouble. You are aware you were trespassing on military property?"

I shake my head and keep staring at my hands.

"I thought it was just an old warehouse. I was just looking for somewhere to sleep. I'm sorry." I look up from my hands. "Please, just let me go. I didn't see anything."

"A lot of trouble to go to, for somewhere to sleep," he observes, steepling his hands and looking at me over the top of his fingertips.

"I thought no one would look for me there."

He pounces on my choice of words immediately. "Who is looking for you?"

"Please…" I look away.

"Who is looking for you?" he demands again, louder. A hand slaps down on the table and I jump.

"I don't know their names. They said if I went to the police, they'd kill me. But now the police are looking for me too."

Morel narrows his eyes. "What did you see?"

"I saw him kill someone."

"So you expect me to believe that you ran away, all the way to France, with no money and no passport? Do you take me for a fool?"

"I fell asleep at the station and someone stole my bag."

"But not your phone." He's sharp. One wrong word and he's going to trip me up.

"It was in my pocket."

"Who were you talking to when my men arrested you?"

I study the cracks in the table instead of answering. I want to just blurt out the whole cover story and get it over with, but I have to drag it out and play for time, as much as I dare.

"If you don't want to answer my questions, I will turn you over to someone who won't ask so nicely."

The thought sends a shudder through me, and I quickly revise my plans about playing for time.

"He's a cop," I tell the table top. "From England. He wants me to go back. He says he can protect me."

"And do you believe he can?"

"I believe he believes he can," I answer carefully.

"And what is his name, this English policeman you do not trust?"

"Sam Yates."

He nods and fixes me with a piercing stare.

"If you have been dishonest about anything, tell me now before we speak to this policeman of yours."

"I'm telling you the truth, I swear."

"I will not give you another chance," he warns. My heart skips a beat, but I can't change my story now.

"I'm not lying," I insist, some of my frustration at this whole damned situation leaking into my voice. "I ran because I was scared. I didn't mean to trespass in your stupid compound!"

"Very well. We shall see." He nods at the soldier guarding the door, who slips silently from the room. They obviously don't intend to waste any time.

A moment later the door swings open again and I turn anxiously in my seat, dreading the soldier telling Morel that my story doesn't check out. It takes me a moment to process what I'm seeing. Outlined in the doorway is Scott, with Nathan beside him. Behind them, Helen is whispering into the ear of the French soldier.

"What is the meaning of this?" Morel demands, rising to his feet.

Helen brushes past Scott, and Morel fixes his eyes on her.

"You need to take a bathroom break," Helen tells him, before he can say another word.

"I..." he starts, with an uncomfortable look on his face. "If you will excuse me, Mademoiselle."

"Of course. And Colonel," she says, reaching out to touch his arm. "You will not allow anyone to stop us leaving this base."

"N– no, of course not," he stammers beneath her fierce glare. "No-one will stop you."

"Good."

He hurries past us, out of the door. Scott is by my side in an instant.

"Anna, are you okay?"

I nod numbly. He takes my arm and helps me from my chair – my legs are suddenly weak, and I can't get up by myself. Helen turns her attention to the soldier who let them in, who has waited silently during the exchange. His eyes appear glazed as he stares blankly ahead.

"Now, Andre, would you be so kind as to escort us out?"

We hurry along behind them, Scott's hand never leaving my arm, and Nathan bringing up the rear. All the while Helen is talking in hushed tones in the soldier's ear. The corridors twist and turn, but we navigate them with ease thanks to our guide. My heart is pounding as I strain to hear the footsteps of anyone pursuing us, and both Scott and Nathan have their pistols drawn. At last we reach the exit and emerge into the grey daylight. Helen whispers one last instruction to the soldier, and then we're in the car and heading for home.

Chapter Thirteen

I don't remember much of the journey home, only that Scott insisted Nathan drive so he could sit in the back with me. I know I cried a lot, and I know he tried to comfort me, but I don't remember any of the words spoken, nor the conversation that passed between Helen and Nathan – apparently he's her new handler. I remember protesting when we arrived back at Langford House, but Scott had insisted I went straight to see Doctor Harwood, telling me it was best to get it out of the way.

I thought I was all cried out by the time I got into her office, but I was wrong. Unlike Scott, though, she doesn't try to comfort me, but has me analyse every word I use to recount the whole horrible mess, which in itself I find comforting. By the time we're finished some two hours later, I'm drained, both mentally and physically.

At last I shuffle out into the hallway to find Scott waiting for me, and my heart reacts in a way I can't quite justify. I try to find the words to thank him for everything he has done – everything he's still doing – but as my eyes meet his, I realise they aren't needed. I offer him a weak smile, and he nods in return.

"Okay, Anna, one more stop then I can get you home."

I'm shaking my head before he's finished speaking.

"No way. I'm done."

"It's up to you, Anna, but Toby has been in pieces."

"He blames himself?" I don't need to wait for his answer. Of course Toby blames himself. And of course I have to go and see him. I nod even as my eyes close of their own accord.

"Okay, let's go."

We find Toby in the lab – where else? – slumped over his desk, but on hearing our footsteps he leaps to his feet, wringing his hands.

"Anna, I'm so sorry, we didn't know, I never thought – we never would have – none of us would ever–"

"Toby, stop," I cut across him, taking his hands in mine. "It wasn't your fault."

"Yes, it was," he says, staring at my feet from behind his shaggy hair. "We should have known something like this could happen; we should have run more simulations. But none of us imagined you'd be able to shift so far..."

"Of course you didn't," I placate him, sounding more relaxed about the whole thing than I feel. "We had no idea what I could do. But now we know. So next time–"

"Anna, no," he says, looking up at me sharply.

"Yes," I say firmly, then soften my tone. "I've got a theory, and I need you to help me test it."

"That's not a good idea," he says, breaking eye contact and pulling his hands from mine. "You need someone better qualified."

"There is no one better qualified," I insist. "Tomorrow, okay?"

*

"So, what's this theory of yours?" Scott asks, as I let us into my flat. He insisted on taking me right to my door, and for once I'm not complaining. For one thing, I'm too tired, but, honestly, I don't want to be alone right now. Every time I closed my eyes, I see French Special Forces advancing on me with their ugly, black weapons drawn.

"Put the kettle on and I'll tell you."

"Deal," he says, disappearing into my tiny kitchen while I tug the shoes from my feet and flop onto the sofa, exhausted.

We talk into the early hours, long after we're both yawning, discussing the merits of my theory and looking for flaws in it. Somewhere along the way the coffee becomes wine, and we're reaching the bottom of the second bottle when he glances up at the clock on the wall.

"I'd best call a cab," he says with a frown, placing his glass on the table.

"Don't," I say, reaching out and putting my hand on his arm as he starts to rise. "Stay."

"Anna..." he says, searching my eyes. "It's been a long day, we've both been drinking..."

"I don't want to be on my own. Just hold me," I say in a small voice, looking down at my feet as I feel my cheeks redden. "Please."

I feel him settle back into the sofa and wrap his arm around my shoulders. I lean my head against his chest and tuck my feet up under me, and that's the last thing I remember.

*

The heavenly scent of fried eggs and bacon seeks me out in my bed. I smile dreamily, then frown as I remember yesterday's events. The glucose pill. France. Me begging Scott to stay. Oh, God. I groan and pull the covers over my head. How embarrassing. At least I didn't sleep with him, I console myself. At least, I don't think I did – truth be told, much of last night is a blur. Oh, God.

Reluctantly I emerge from beneath the duvet, wrap a dressing gown around myself and pad barefoot through the living room. I pause as I see a bed made up on the sofa, and smile. Of course Scott is too much of a gentleman to have taken advantage of me last night. I just hope I didn't make too much of a fool of myself.

His voice drifts towards me, and the hushed tones make me hesitate.

"Don't worry, I have it in hand. She trusts me. I've got to go."

My bliss shattered, I backtrack quickly to the bedroom and quietly push the door shut before perching on the edge of the bed. I need a moment to process what I just heard. I'm sure I'm overreacting; it can't be what it seemed. Because it seemed a lot like Scott was admitting to manipulating me. I shake my head, scattering the thought. That's madness. After everything he did for me yesterday – if he bore me any ill will whatsoever, all he had to do was take a little longer to reach me.

Of course, that wouldn't have been in AbGen's best interest, the little voice niggles at me. I'd be of no use to them in the hands of the French. That was assuming he was even talking to AbGen. Who knows who else wants to get their hands on my ability, and what they would pay for it?

"Stop it," I tell myself firmly, meeting my own gaze in the mirror at the bottom of my bed. I'm being stupid. The man saved my life yesterday and I'm doubting him based on what? The tail end of an over-heard conversation? There could be any number of explanations for what he said. And besides, my ability isn't worth a thing to anyone without my cooperation.

"So stop being so paranoid," I mutter to myself in disgust. I already decided to trust Scott, and that means giving him the benefit of the doubt, and not just when it suits me. I resolve not to even ask him about it. In fact, I'm going to forget the whole thing. It's not important anymore, anyway. I've made some decisions, and I'm pretty sure Scott isn't going to like them.

I jump in the shower before grabbing some clean clothes from the wardrobe and tidying my hair. Bad enough that he saw me in the state I was in last night; I'm not going to let him see me looking like something the cat dragged in this morning. I didn't waste the time, using it to think over my decision and make sure I'm a hundred percent certain. I am.

I push open the bedroom door, making enough noise to ensure I don't disturb any more private conversations. I needn't have worried, I can see Scott moving around the kitchen, no phones in sight.

"Morning, sleepyhead," he greets me with a smile, putting two plates laden with food on the kitchen table, where two steaming mugs are already waiting.

"What time is it?" I ask with a frown, settling into my seat. With all the confusion this morning I haven't gotten around to putting my watch on, but now that he mentions it, it does feel later than my usual rising time.

"Just gone ten," he says, confirming my suspicions. "You needed it after the day you had yesterday. Don't worry, I've told Langford we'll be in late."

166

"Yeah, about that..." I start, playing with my fork and noticing the water stains on it from where I didn't dry it properly last time I used it. Something in my tone makes Scott put his cutlery down and focus his full attention on me. I can feel his curious look burning into me, and picture the frown on his face. With a sigh, I set the fork down and look across at him.

"I'm not going back," I announce, and carry on before he can argue. "After what happened yesterday.... it's just too dangerous. I can't."

"I understand," he says, and it's my turn to frown. That's not the reaction I'd been expecting. At all. As ever, Scott seems to sense my confusion.

"Anna, no one's going to force you to do something you don't want to do, and you're right, it is dangerous. None of us fully understand this ability of yours. But..." He pauses, either to choose his words or make sure he has my full attention, I'm not sure which. "Don't you want to? Your ability is dangerous whether we're helping you or not. And at least with AbGen behind you, you're not on your own if something goes wrong. Like yesterday."

I shudder, picturing myself in France, knowing no one is coming to help. Scott makes a compelling argument. But I shake my head.

"I know enough to stop myself shifting. That's all I need. I'll lock it away, never use it again. It's the safest way."

"If that's what you want, I'll support you, you know that. But just think about it – don't rush into anything, okay?"

I bite my tongue and nod instead of disagreeing. It's a reasonable enough request, much as it goes against my instinct. After everything he's done for me, I owe him this much at least. And maybe I am being a little hasty.

"Okay, I'll give it until the end of the week," I reluctantly agree, and turn my attention to the eggs and bacon in front of me to discover I've lost my appetite.

Chapter Fourteen

G rab her from behind. Get your arm around her throat."

It's not as bad as it sounds – I'm being trained in hand-to-hand combat. I've been having self-defence lessons every morning since joining AbGen, and it turns out I have a bit of a flair for it, which surprises no one so much as me. Of course, it's not much help against half a dozen armed soldiers, but it's nice to know I'm not utterly useless at everything I turn my hand to.

I hear Scott moving behind me as he gets into position, locks his right forearm around my throat and grips my t-shirt with his hand, pinning me tightly against him. His grip is loose enough that I can breathe, but the pressure is not insignificant and there's no way I could get free by struggling. He knows better than to go easy on me: not much gets by Nick, the resident hand-to-hand combat instructor. We're both aching from the long session – me from the heavy workout, and Scott from being thrown around like a ragdoll for the better part of an hour – but neither of us is prepared to ease up.

"Grab his right hand with your left, putting pressure here and here," Nick tells me, pointing out two spots on Scott's hand. I glance down at the spots and nod as much as Scott's grip will allow me. "You're going to twist his hand and put pressure on the wrist until his grip gives out, then push the hand up behind his back to lock up the elbow. Once his upper body is immobilised, step in with your foot in the back of his knee here–" He taps the point on the back of my own knee "–and push forward and down. Take the arm with him as he goes down so you can hold him there."

I nod, absorbing the information and running it through my head. Grip hand, twist, raise hand, foot on back of knee. Got it.

"Obviously in a real-life situation you'd use an elbow strike or a headbutt to loosen his grip first, but we won't do that here."

"Yes, please let's not do that here," Scott interjects.

"Wimp," I mutter with a smirk.

"We'll see who's the wimp," he murmurs back, tightening his grip on my throat.

I grip his hand and squeeze, grinning in triumph as his fingers loosen. I twist it, bringing all my force to bear on his wrist – it's harder than Nick made it sound – and manage to pull it off. A quick step puts me behind him, and I hear him grunt as I twist his elbow up. I push my foot into the back of his knee, and he hits the mat with a satisfying thud. I release his wrist and smile angelically.

"It's still you."

"Ha. Ha," he says, rolling onto his back and massaging his wrist. I offer my hand to help him to his feet and he reaches out for it. I'm going to miss these sessions when I leave AbGen. Sure, I could always take classes somewhere else, but it just won't be the same if I'm not training with Scott.

There's a sudden pressure around my wrist and before I know what's happening, I'm face down on the mat with my arm twisted up behind me and Scott straddling me.

"Hey, no fair!" I complain. "We haven't covered that yet."

He laughs and climbs off me, then helps me up.

"Once more," Nick instructs.

We reset our positions and Scott grabs me from behind again. This time I dislodge his hand much more easily, and it's only a matter of seconds before he thuds face first into the mat again.

"Excellent, Anna," Nick praises. "Let's leave it there for today."

"Yeah," Scott echoes, rubbing his wrist. "Let's leave it there for today."

We grab some water then hit the showers, and make our way down to the firing range, where Scott has scheduled my first lesson with the resident firearms specialist. It's as if he's on a personal crusade to prove to me that I'm safer with AbGen. Maybe he's right. But funnily enough, nothing about the idea of holding a gun makes me feel any safer.

"Hi Anna, I'm Dominic Fletcher. Everyone calls me Fletch." The short, balding firearms instructor extends a hand to me and I shake it tentatively, looking behind him to the large, mostly empty room. A yellow and black line runs across the varnished wooden floor from one side to the other, and beyond it on the far wall is a row of human-shaped targets, each hanging from a motorised clip. Tracks run along the ceiling, presumably for moving the targets closer or further away.

"So, we're going to get you acquainted with the basics today. First things first: ear protectors. Any time you're on the range, you need to wear these."

He hands me a pair of distinctly unstylish earmuffs – another reason to avoid spending too much time down here. Scott gets a pair too, which is some consolation. At least I don't have to look like a weirdo by myself. Fletch pulls a key on a chain from around his neck and uses it to unlock a wire-doored cage that's fitted to the wall. Running from the ground to head height, it's filled with row upon row of guns. I recognise the shotguns and rifles, though I've never seen one up close before, but it's a pistol Fletch reaches for.

"This is a SIG-Sauer P228 9mm semi-automatic pistol, the weapon of choice for most of the agents here. You're welcome to use one of these until you're assigned your own."

He slides the top back and checks inside, then tilts the gun and checks the bottom.

"Always make sure the weapon is made safe – no magazine and no round in the chamber – before handing it to someone or storing it away."

He hands the gun to me – it's heavier than I was expecting and I stare at the weighty lump of metal for a long moment. To think that this thing is capable of killing, and that I might one day have to use it against someone… a shudder runs through me. If Fletch notices, he doesn't say anything. I fight the urge to hand it right back and instead focus on the matte-black metal and feeling the textured grip as it sits in my hand. Some part of me acknowledges that for a killing machine it's kind of beautiful… in a macabre sort of way.

"Wrap your right hand around the grip, like this, and support it with your left hand, under here."

He arranges my hands, and immediately my outstretched arms feel the pressure. This stance is going to take some getting used to – not that I really want to get used to it.

"Keep your finger outside of the trigger guard until you're ready to fire."

I nod, and move my finger away from the trigger, resting it lightly on the outside of the trigger guard. It doesn't feel any safer.

"Okay, now you're going to load it. Remember: never point your weapon at something you're not willing to shoot."

I nod again and try to banish the image of an innocent bystander hurt by one of my bullets. Fletch hands me a rectangular piece of metal and I can see the bullets sitting inside it.

"This is your magazine. Slide it inside the magazine well," he says, indicating to the bottom of the gun, "and wiggle it gently inside until you feel it click."

I ease it inside, trying to keep my fingers well away from the trigger, and Fletch nods his approval.

"Now pull back the slide with your left hand and then take up your stance again. The weapon is now cocked and loaded."

With the loaded weapon in my hands, everything suddenly seems a lot more real. I swallow noisily and stay very still.

"When you're ready, release the safety with your thumb, then line up the front and rear sights with that target. Take a deep breath, release it, and then gently squeeze the trigger."

The gun wrenches in my hands and there's a loud bang that deafens me even through the earmuffs, and then a metallic ping. The two sounds echo around the room. I look down the barrel of the gun – which is no longer pointing where I aimed it – and search for a bullet hole in the humanoid target. Nothing. I hear a faint chuckle from Scott and glance back at him over my shoulder, taking care to keep the gun pointed down the range. He nods at the next target along, and I see my bullet lodged in the upper right corner. Not only have I missed my own target, I've missed it by so much that I caught the one in the next lane.

"Congratulations," Fletch says with a wry grin. "You've just hit Mrs Jones on her way back from the supermarket. Let's give it another go."

That's the last thing I want to do, but I can see there's no way I'm getting off that lightly. With a grimace, I raise the pistol again and line it up with the target. My second shot isn't much better, and nor is the one after. Fletch adjusts my position.

"Try to stay relaxed and don't anticipate the recoil. Keep your grip loose. You're tensing up as you pull the trigger."

175

I don't see how loosening my grip on the gun is going to stop it leaping all over the place as it goes off, but I nod anyway and try to follow his instructions. By the time I've fired another thirty or so shots and reloaded twice, my bullets are hitting the right target, but that's the best that can be said for any of my attempts. The holes in the sheet are completely erratic – some high, some wide, and a couple low. The only real consistency is that none of them have actually landed inside the crudely drawn outline of a person.

"I think your gun is a pacifist." I hold the weapon out to Fletch and hope I never have to use one for real. It's safe to say that we're all better off when I don't have a loaded gun in my hands.

Fletch laughs. "You'll get the hang of it. Come back and see me tomorrow."

I wonder if there's a way I can get out of it without offending him, but there's something else playing on my mind as we leave. I broach the subject with Scott as we're walking down one of the long corridors.

"What happens if we're carrying guns and we get arrested? I mean, they're pretty illegal, right?" It's not like I could pull out an ID card and tell the cops it's okay because I work for AbGen, given that its existence is a state secret.

"If you ever get picked up, use your phone call to contact Gardiner. He'll have you out in no time."

I frown, picturing myself locked in a cell with Gardiner my only hope of salvation. The image does not sit well with me. I'm so lost in my thoughts that I don't realise where we're going. Until I do.

"What are we doing here?" I demand, narrowing my eyes. Sandra's door looms at the end of the corridor.

"I thought it might be a good idea to talk to someone impartial, before you make your decision."

"She's hardly impartial," I object. "I might as well speak to Gardiner himself."

"Actually, that's not a bad idea."

"Are you kidding me? He's the last person I can trust."

"Anna, enough! What more has the man got to do to prove he's on your side?"

Scott looks just as riled as I am. I realise that he's put up with a lot from me over the last few weeks, and now I'm running down the man he's looked up to for the last seven years. But I can't help myself. Gardiner makes my skin crawl, and I grind my teeth in frustration. I don't get this absolute faith Scott has in him.

"Something isn't right," I snap at him. "Why can't you see that – are you blind? He can't be trusted!"

Scott grabs my shoulders roughly and pushes me against the wall. My mouth goes bone dry and my heart hammers in my chest. His jaw is clenched, and he's breathing heavily – I've never seen him this angry and suddenly this whole conversation seems like a really bad idea. Especially in an empty corridor. I've got no idea what he's capable of. I struggle ineffectively: he's too strong and his fingers are digging into my shoulders and his eyes are boring into mine.

"He saved my life, okay?" I stop struggling and stare at him. "He saved me."

*

"It was during a dark period of my life."

We're sitting in a deserted corner of the canteen, feigning interest in our cooling coffees, and Scott is steadfastly avoiding eye contact.

"I've never really explained how my ability works, have I?" he says. I shake my head but say nothing.

"When I get anywhere within about ten miles of an absa, I'm drawn to them." He shakes his head. "Drawn isn't a strong enough word. It's like... like an obsession. A compulsion. I have to find them, have to be near them. It's all I can think about. More important than food, more important than sleep... nothing else matters. Can you understand that, Anna? Nothing."

178

I can't even begin to imagine how it must feel to be taken over like that. I remember my first day here when I was under Helen's thrall, and try to imagine what it must be like to feel that way permanently. A shudder runs through me. Scott sees it and nods.

"It was a little over seven years ago when I first crossed paths with the woman – an absa. We think that's what triggered my talent. Of course, I didn't know what it was back then, all I knew was that I had to be around her. So, I followed her. I didn't sleep for two days, I couldn't eat, I just kept watching her – when she was at home, when she went to work... I couldn't stay away."

He picks up a spoon and stirs his coffee, and I feel a stab of sympathy. He's never talked about his past before, now I know why.

"She had a fiancé, a huge guy, ex-army. He came after me and warned me off, told me to disappear or he'd make me – permanently. I knew he could do it, but I didn't care. Being away from her was worse than being dead."

He breaks off and looks across at me.

"Understand that I was completely on my own. I didn't have the upbringing you might imagine, and by the time this was happening, I had no one – I'd long since lost contact with my family, I was in and out of trouble with the law so I never stayed in one place long enough to make friends. I knew what I was doing wasn't right, I knew something was wrong with me, but I had no-one to talk it through with."

He takes a deep breath and then lets it out again while I try to imagine what it must be like to be so utterly alone in the world. I don't have much family, just my mum, but we were always close, and even now she's only ever a phone call away.

"I tried to stay away, but it was like she was the only thing that existed in my world. She moved a few miles away, but not far enough. I could still sense her, and it didn't take me long to track her down. A couple of days later, the fiancé came for me again, but he made the mistake of coming alone. He was stronger than me, and better trained, but I was desperate. We were both in a bad way by the time we finished, but I wasn't going to let anything stand between me and her... I'd kill him first. And that's when I realised. I couldn't sense her anymore. She was gone. He'd sent her away before he came after me. I was furious. I turned on him again, but I had a moment of clarity. Away from her, I could think again. I called him an ambulance, then dragged myself up to the top of a nearby building. I had to make sure I never hurt anyone else, I couldn't lose control like that again. I climbed up on the ledge–"

He's blinking furiously and taking rapid breaths. His hand is gripping the table so hard that his knuckles have turned white. I reach over and place my hand on top of his, squeezing it softly. His grip loosens and he gives me a lopsided smile.

"That's where Gardiner found me, out on that ledge. He told me what I was, what the girl was – they'd been tracking her too – and he brought me in. It was hard at first, being surrounded by so many absas, but he helped me learn to control it, and showed me I could use my talent to help people, not hurt them."

He takes a sip of his coffee, grimaces, and sets it aside.

"So now you know why I trust him," he says. I nod.

"I'm sorry. I promise I'll try to trust him too. And I'm sorry for what you went through."

"Anna, I'm the one who should be apologising. I should never have reacted that way. I truly am sorry – can you forgive me?"

"Of course," I answer easily, and add softly, "You're *my* Gardiner."

Scott smiles. "I hope that's a compliment. Come on, we both need some air. Let's get out of here."

Chapter Fifteen

S omething looks different."

It's the day after I told Scott I wanted to quit, and so far I haven't, which he seems to be taking as a victory. After hearing about what he went through, I can't help but feel that I might be overreacting. If he could learn to control something that erased everything he was, something that would drive him to kill, then surely I can learn to control this. What I know for sure is that I'm at least going to try, and hence we're back in the lab, ready to test my theory. Toby hasn't asked why I didn't show yesterday, which makes me wonder if he already knows – AbGen takes office gossip to a whole new level – or if he thought that whole France thing caught up with me, which wouldn't be entirely untrue. I'm terrified of where I might end up if my theory is wrong, but determined not to show it, and adamant that it's not going to stop me trying. We've just come into the EM-shielded room, and something looks... well, different.

"We've fitted EM sensors into the walls," Toby says. "Mr Gardiner wants us to measure the strength of the pulse you emit when you shift."

"Why?" I ask, my concerns about Gardiner immediately resurfacing. Is he thinking about trying to weaponise my ability? Perhaps my earlier suspicions about his intentions weren't entirely unfounded.

I see Scott shoot me a look and remember my promise about trying to trust AbGen's commander. I raise my hands in mock surrender before he can say anything.

"Just curious."

"Sorry, Anna," Toby says, oblivious as ever to the tension in the room. "You'd have to ask him; I just do what I'm told."

I nod, resolving to do exactly that. First things first though, I have a theory to test. There's a desk wedged in one corner of the room, and on top of it sits a single bottle of glucose tablets, next to a timer set for ten minutes. I shake out one of the pills and stare at it, trying to blot France from my memory.

"Are you alright, Anna?" Scott asks, quietly enough that Toby can't hear him. I nod, not trusting myself to speak.

"You don't have to do this."

"Yeah, I do," I say, my voice a hoarse whisper. If I don't do it now, I never will. I put the pill in my mouth and start to chew. As an afterthought, I shake out another and put it in my pocket, just in case. Scott puts his hand on my shoulder and gives it a gentle squeeze, and I flash back to the night before last, curled up on the sofa together. He'll keep me safe, I know he will.

Toby hits a button on the timer and it starts to count down.

"So, run me through this theory again," Toby says as Scott steers me firmly into the only seat in the room before I can start to pace, and my foot immediately starts tapping on the concrete flooring. I make a conscious effort to stop it and focus on Toby's question.

"Okay, so every time I've shifted intentionally, I've made myself afraid until my ability kicks in, right? And every time I've accidentally shifted, I've been genuinely afraid. But there's one thing that's different about the very first time I shifted – I didn't just want to escape, I wanted to be back safe at home. Every other time, I've just wanted to get as far away as possible."

"That's why you ended up in France – because our pill let you go further?" I can hear the guilt in his voice as he puts it together. "Anna, I'm so—"

"Nope, don't say it," I cut him off, because this room is claustrophobic enough without making space for his guilt and my anxiety. "No more apologies, okay?" He nods but looks unhappy. After a moment, he perks up again.

"So you're just going to click your heels and think of home?"

"That's the plan."

"Then whenever you're ready, Dorothy."

I grimace – that had better not be my new nickname – and close my eyes. I let my awareness of the lab fall away and focus on the growing knot of fear inside me. It creeps up through my stomach and burns up through my lungs until it's bubbling in my throat, threatening to drown me and I can't think of anything else. All I know is I have to get out of here, I need to get home, I've got to–

*

"Sir, Anna," Joe greets us as we step inside Langford House. He'd tried the whole ma'am thing with me at first, but it made me feel forty, so I set him straight on that score. I'm twenty-one for crying out loud – I'm *much* too young to be a ma'am. I mean, honestly, do I look like a ma'am?

"You're never going to let that go, are you?" he asks with a smile, while Scott shoots a confused look in my direction, and I make a mental note to watch my thoughts around the mind reader. The overly nosy mind reader, I add for Joe's benefit.

"Hey, just making sure I stay sharp."

He seems plenty sharp to me already.

"Why thank you, ma'am," he says, a boyish grin tugging at the corners of his mouth. Seriously, you'd never believe his talent takes absolute concentration; he makes it look so natural. If he heard that, he makes no comment on it, but I know he can't hold that level of focus for long.

Scott finishes checking in with Nora and we step into the lift.

"Canteen?" he suggests, his finger hovering over the control panel, and my stomach rumbles in response. I'm starting to suspect this man knows me a little too well. The shift went brilliantly. I ended up just two miles from home, and we're going to need to check it on a map, but it looks like I travelled more or less in a straight line. It's the first time I've felt like I've really had some control over my talent, and I like it. But as always, shifting has left me ravenous. I hope it uses a lot of calories, because otherwise these extra meals are going to start showing.

As the lift doors slide open, I reach a decision.

"Bathroom break. I'll catch you up."

It's not that I don't trust him – honestly, it's not – but I don't think he'd approve of what I have in mind, especially after our chat yesterday. The EM sensors in the training room have me on edge. There's something not right there, and it's like Toby said: if I want to know why they're there, I need to speak to Gardiner. I'm not going back on my word about trusting him, not really. I mean, there's nothing wrong in wanting to know what he's got planned, right? I'm sure there's a perfectly reasonable explanation for what he's doing and why he didn't bother to tell me. Yeah.

"Uh, Anna?" Scott's voice interrupts my reverie. "The bathroom's that way."

He nods in the opposite direction to the one I'd been going in. I laugh awkwardly and head back past him. From the corner of my eye, I see him shake his head and walk away. I push open the third door on the right and step into the ladies. The room is small and barren. There aren't many restrooms that can make The Glasshouse's look classy, but this is one of them. In fact, its sole redeeming feature is that right now it's empty. I loiter and try to work out how long it'll take Scott to get down the corridor and into the lift. After counting to thirty, I poke my head into the corridor and glance around cautiously. The coast is clear. I hurry back along it. I won't have long before Scott starts wondering where I am, and this isn't a conversation I want to have with him.

I step into the lift that leads to Gardiner's elaborate office, tapping my foot as it makes its way oh so slowly to where I need to be. After what seems like an age, the door opens and I step out, by which time I've already started to wonder if this is a good idea. Gardiner isn't likely to take kindly to me questioning him and I don't know what he's capable of, not truly. But he saved Scott's life, and that's got to count for something. I raise my hand and rap on his door before I can completely lose my nerve.

"Come," a voice instructs from inside. As I swing the door open and cross the threshold, Gardiner looks up from behind his desk, pen in hand.

"Anna, what can I do for you?" he asks.

"Is… is this a good time?" I ask, my nerve deserting me the moment his reptilian eyes fix on my face.

"Of course. Please, sit," he says with a smile that makes me want to back away, whilst gesturing to the chair in front of his gargantuan desk. I sink into it, and shuffle awkwardly. This must be what it was like for kids at school who were summoned to see the headmaster. Except I'm the one who chose to be here, not the other way around.

"I notice you've fitted some sensors in the EM room," I say, a little more bluntly than I'd intended. If Gardiner is surprised by my knowledge of this it doesn't show, even though I'm scrutinising his face closely. But reading faces isn't really my thing. I sure wouldn't mind Joe's talent right about now.

"I did," he says with a slight nod, setting his pen aside.

"Toby says they're there to measure the EMP I give off when I shift?"

"That's correct."

It looks like I'm going to have to do all the legwork in this conversation if I want it to go anywhere.

"I was just wondering…" I start, and then pause. "Why is it you wanted to measure that?"

Instead of answering, he presses a button on his intercom.

"Page Doctor Pearce to my office, please."

I raise an eyebrow at him and wonder if he's deliberately avoiding my question. And who the hell still uses pagers?

"He can help clarify," he explains. I'm obviously not at Gardiner's level when it comes to concealing my emotions. "But in the meantime, I'll do my best. As I'm sure you're aware, Anna, your EM Pulse can cause considerable damage to technology."

I nod. Scott has already told me that on my first attempt in the lab I took all of Langford House's computers offline, and my phone shuts down every time I shift. None of this makes me feel any better about where this conversation is going. Gardiner is scrutinising me closely though, so I try to make a better job of keeping my face blank.

"Have you ever stopped to think what that means?"

"It means I work in an EM shielded room," I say, working to keep my voice even. "So I don't do any more damage to our equipment."

"Well yes, that's true," he agrees. "But what if we weren't just talking about our equipment?"

"I don't–" I shake my head, trying to imagine any way this isn't heading where I think it is.

"Have you ever lain awake wondering what would happen should one of our enemies in the Middle East acquire a nuclear warhead and decide to launch an attack against us? Or if North Korea launches an airstrike on the scale of the Blitz, only instead of archaic bombers, they utilised all of the technology at their disposal?"

The change of subject throws me and I'm not sure how to respond. While I'm groping for words, the door clicks open behind me and Walter Pearce steps unobtrusively into the room. Gardiner pays him no heed.

"No, I don't suppose you have. You're young, and the young are often short-sighted when they look to the future. But you see, I have, Ms Mason, and I am acutely aware of the fragility of our nation."

Gardiner leans forward in his chair, his intense stare boring into me.

"Anna, the potential for what you can do to serve your country is incredible; perhaps greater than any one person who has ever been born to our nation. And what about your colleagues? If one of them were to be captured, you could save them simply by shifting and neutralising all of the enemy's equipment. Is that not something you would want?"

He's not wrong, but…

"You're talking about weaponising my ability," I state, finally verbalising my fear. Gardiner says nothing, watching me as I process this turn of events. Truth be told, it doesn't take much processing. Ever since he recruited me, I'd expected something like this, dreaded something like this. I'd seen it in his eyes on that very first day.

"Yes, Anna," he says at length. "I'm talking about weaponising your ability. But this isn't something to fear: don't you see the potential?"

All I see is an aging guy in a suit, staring at a weapon locked inside an inconvenient human form. I don't like the idea of being a weapon. I don't like the idea of being anything, other than a small-town waitress.

"I think it's time for me to leave," I say, my voice quivering. I push myself up from the chair, almost knocking it over in my haste. I reach the door and pull it open.

"Anna, please," Gardiner says, a frown creasing his face. "Calm down. Let's not make any hasty decisions. We can talk this through."

I'm already shaking my head. I don't want to talk this through, not with him. There's only one person I want to speak to right now, and he's waiting for me in the canteen. Or do I? The thought pulls me up. He's one of them. He's the one who's been working so hard to convince me to stay. In my confusion, I almost miss Gardiner nod over my shoulder at Pearce. I turn in time to see the scientist looming over me.

"What's that?" I say, staring at the syringe in his hand, rooted helplessly to the spot. He jabs it into my arm and presses the plunger before I can regain the use of my legs.

"Hey, get off me!" I try to twist away but his hand locks around my upper arm. I struggle against him with no effect, and Gardiner strides from behind his desk and closes the gap between us.

"What are you doing?" I demand, but my voice comes out closer to scared than indignant. "What was that?"

"That, Anna," Gardiner says, calmly taking my other arm so I am completely trapped, "is a fast-acting insulin that will rapidly deplete any glucose in your system. I've just clipped your wings."

"What? No, you can't…!" I struggle harder, but his grip is biting into my upper arm and I can already feel the poison working its way through my system, slowing me down, making it hard to think straight. My limbs are sluggish and not reacting to my commands the way they should. I turn my hand over and stare at the outstretched fingers, blurred around the edges. I should fight back before they… because they... I need to…

Ow! I gasp, and air rasps along my throat. The burning in my head, my head is…. It hurts, and my stomach is twisting. I know this feeling, I've just shifted. No, someone's holding me, *he's* holding me, he's a bad man. It burns. It's getting worse. Hypoglycaemia. That's what Toby said it was. Toby. My shining knight. He made me a magic pill. The pill. Something about the pill, the thought is dancing just out of reach, leaping away before I can catch it. The pill, the pill, the pill… It's in my pocket! I grasp the thought with a moment of crystal clarity. My right arm is free, and Gardiner is… I don't know, doing something at the wall. It doesn't matter. I can get to the pill. I reach into my pocket as slowly as I dare – I don't know how long this lucidity will last, but Pearce is still on my left – and my fingers curl around the pill. It's smooth and oblong, it feels cool against my palm. So smooth, pretty bead. No, it's a pill, the pill, I have to take it. My hand floats through the air and presses it through my lips. Lips. Soft and squishy, I run my finger across them.

"…get her into the lift before…"

"…lower dosage…"

The words float around me and then I'm moving forward towards the wall, my feet stumbling over each other but the hands stop me falling. Oh. There's a hole in the wall. A room, a room behind the wall. Was that always there? We're inside it now, the voices are still talking, and two sliding doors start to close. Through the gap I see Scott staring in at me, and then the doors press together and the room starts to move downwards.

"Where…?" I try to ask, but I don't know if the words make it past my lips.

"We have a place for people like you." It's Gardiner's voice, and I frown as I stare at his lips, trying to focus on his words. "People who need an… adjustment to their attitude."

His words are getting easier to follow, and I feel the lift jolt to a stop with a loud buzz.

"Please… lemme go," I mutter, letting my words slur and run together, and sagging in their arms.

"Oh no, Anna, it's a bit late for that. And I'm afraid you're not going to like what comes next."

The doors slide open, and he's not wrong. The stark lighting sends new bolts of fire screaming through my skull, and I want to screw my eyes shut against it, but I can't bring myself to look away from the horror in front of me.

Archaic metal devices and chains line one of the walls; a telltale blood stain on the otherwise bare concrete leaves no ambiguity as to their purpose. The air is thick with the stench of pain and fear – even through this insulin-induced fog there is no mistaking it.

I don't have time to get my bearings before they are dragging me from the lift and marching me across the room. Half a dozen cages line the other wall, with metal bars running from floor to ceiling. As we pass the first of them, I catch a glimpse of a figure watching us from inside. She's curled up in the far corner, her arms wrapped around her knees, apparently resigned to her fate. Her dirty-blonde hair hangs around her pale face in dull, tangled waves. Her t-shirt is faded and her blue jeans stop just short of her bare feet, but it's her eyes that make my stomach churn.

A coldness creeps up my spine. If I don't do something, that's going to be me. I can still feel the insulin pumping through my veins; I've never shifted in this condition, I don't even know if I can. I'm torn – try to shift now and take my chances, or wait for the pill to fully kick in and risk them discovering my deception.

"Marcus, activate the EM disruptor. We wouldn't want Anna leaving us before she has a chance to sample our hospitality."

"Yes, sir."

I just catch myself from turning to follow the sound of the new voice – I hadn't seen anyone else here when we got out of the lift. He comes from behind me and I watch from the corner of my eye as he approaches a small silver-grey cylindrical device and flicks a switch. Immediately a whirring starts up and a red light flashes on its display panel.

"It takes a little under two minutes to activate," Pearce tells Gardiner. "I've tuned it specifically to Anna's electro-magnetic frequency. Once it's fully active, she won't be able to shift until you turn it off again."

I stare in horror, rooted to the spot. I need to get out of here. Has the pill worked yet? I don't know, but I'm out of time. If they put me in that cage, I'm never coming out again, not as me. I can't let that happen. I've got to get away, I've need to get out of here, I've got to–

Chapter Sixteen

My legs crumple from beneath me, and pain surges through my head, crushing and burning and tearing all at once, hammering behind my eyes like it wants to pop them right out of my skull. I bite back a scream and grab at my head, my fingers tangling in my hair of their own accord, and my every instinct is overwritten by the primal need to make... it... stop!

Breathe. I need to breathe. The realisation comes as a surprise. My lungs are burning and my chest feels like it's being crushed by an iron band, though I'm barely aware of anything beyond the agony in my skull. I gasp the cool air and the pressure lessens. I suck in the air gratefully – I never knew air could taste so sweet – and focus on the sensation. Breathe in, two, three, four. Out, two, three, four, five. In, two, three, four...

I'm not sure how long I sit here just breathing, but eventually the pain in my head recedes enough for me to wonder where 'here' is. I look around – an alleyway, a deserted road, a few grafitti'd tower blocks – and resign myself to the fact that I don't recognise any of them. But at least I'm out. Away from Gardiner, away from the ca–

No, I don't have time to think about that. Falling apart is not a luxury I can afford right now. For all I know,

Gardiner might already have someone on my tail. I need to get moving.

I push myself up off the floor, and immediately trip over my own feet, crashing towards a wall. I raise a hand in time to break my fall and lean against the damp brickwork, catching my breath and waiting for the dizziness to pass. I stumble onwards, keeping my hand against the wall and gasping in the pungent air. Wherever I am, it's not far enough away from Langford House for my liking.

I'm lucky I managed to shift at all. If I didn't have that spare pill in my pocket... It doesn't bear thinking about.

I blink rapidly a few times. I know I have to keep moving – but where? And how am I going to get there? I have nothing with me but the clothes I am wearing and the contents of my pockets. Somehow, I don't feel like going back to Langford House to get my bike and the rest of the stuff stowed in my locker. I keep putting one foot in front of the other, with no idea of where I'm going. The wall falls away behind me and I stagger on without its support, drawing more attention than is probably wise from passers-by. I put them out of my head. By the time word gets back to Langford House, I'll be long gone. Which brings me back to the pressing question. I can't just keep stumbling on aimlessly. I need a plan. I've got to get home, get a change of clothes and some money, and– Go where? Do what? How do you even begin to run from something as big as AbGen? But I have to try, I've got to find a way. I'm not letting them lock me in a cage.

I glance up, almost tripping over a broken paving slab as I do, and spot a corner shop in the distance. I keep hobbling that way, feeling in my pocket for change I left in there. It isn't much, but it will have to do. I need to get rid of this headache so I can think straight. I'm missing something obvious, I know I am, but I just can't–

A bell sounds above my head as I swing open the door and step inside. From behind the counter an old woman eyes me suspiciously and tuts to herself – walking in a straight line is still beyond my ability, and to the casual observer I probably look like I've started early for a night out – but I ignore her and shuffle to the small supply of medications on an end aisle, picking up a pack of paracetamol and heading to the counter. As an afterthought, I grab a chocolate bar and a fizzy drink and dump them on the counter beneath the woman's sneer. I need to raise my sugar levels. She stares at me for a long moment like she's thinking about refusing to serve me – or worse, calling the cops – but eventually she rings up my purchases and accepts my money.

Back out on the street, I eat the chocolate and wash two of the pills down with a mouthful of fizzy drink. I'm not sure how much sugar it's going to take to get my body functional again but I'm not taking any chances, so I force myself to drink the rest of the bottle. A bleep tells me my phone has finally rebooted, so I pull it out and fumble with the maps app. While it loads, I rummage back in my pocket and discover that my worldly wealth amounts to a little under five pounds. Great. How am I going to get home with this?

It turns out the answer is on the phone screen, staring at me next to the flashing blue dot. A train station, just a few streets from here. Perfect. I can buy a ticket to the next stop, ride the train all the way back to Whitelyn, and jump the gate when I get there. I can't afford to get caught or arrested – who knows how far AbGen's influence spreads? – but security is always lapse. It's worth the risk. If I stay here, it's only a matter of time until I'm caught anyway.

The map disappears, and the phone buzzes in my hand. It almost slips right through my shaking fingers. An incoming call from DS Yates. Scott's cover name. I remember his face staring at me as Gardiner and Pearce dragged me from the room. Staring and doing nothing. My heart is thumping all the way up in my throat. What do I do – do I answer? Let it ring? Start running?

I chew my bottom lip and twist my fingers in my hair. Eventually though, curiosity gets the better of me. It can't hurt just to see what he wants, right? I run my tongue over my gums and, against my better judgement, accept the call.

"Hello?" I croak.

Shit. What am I doing? It could be anyone, even Gardiner himself. Not that it matters, I remind myself firmly. They're all the enemy now. So it makes no sense when relief floods through me at the sound of Scott's voice.

"Anna, you're okay. Thank God."

"No thanks to you!" I snap. "You betrayed me."

"I swear I didn't know."

"Bullshit." His voice may be genuine, but I'm not falling for that trick again. "You let them take me, and you did nothing."

"You think I would have gone along with this? Anna, I would never do anything to hurt you, you *know* that. You've got to believe me."

"Well, that's the thing. I don't."

"Anna, I know you're scared, but please, just listen to me." I say nothing, but push myself to my feet and start heading in the direction of the train station. I feel way too vulnerable sitting out here in the open.

"Whatever you do, don't go back to your flat. He's got people there waiting for you."

That stops me dead in my tracks. Of course they've got people waiting for me, that's the first thing he would do. I almost walked right into a trap. I can't believe I was so stupid! But stupid seems to be my thing recently. I loose a frustrated sigh, and my voice comes out somewhere between pleading and bitter.

"I just want everything to go back to how it was… I didn't ask for any of this."

"I know, but you can't think about that now. We've got to keep this short. You took out the base's equipment when you shifted, but it won't be long before its back online. They could be tracking your phone already."

I pull the phone away from my ear and stare at it in horror. Oh, my God. I need to get rid of it before they find me.

"Anna?"

"Yeah. Yeah, I'm here."

"They could be listening in right now, so just say yes or no. Do you remember our first ride?"

"Yes." I'm hardly likely to forget – that was the day we rode out to the lake, and I decided to join AbGen.

"Can you get there?"

"I don't know. Maybe. Yes."

"Good. I'll wait for you there."

The line goes dead. Do I trust him? I don't know. But I don't have any better options right now. I can't go home and I sure as hell can't risk sitting out here in the open. I need to keep moving, and that's as good a direction as any. The train is out, though; there are no stations near where I need to be. I think for a moment, then flag down the first taxi that passes.

"I've got to get to Ryebridge," I tell him. "Please, I'm desperate. I don't have any money, but I'll give you my phone."

The third driver I stop looks undecided. I can see on his face he thinks it's stolen, but it's obviously been a quiet day for him.

"Please, I need to get away from my boyfriend," I fabricate. "He... he–" The day's events catch up with me and tears well up more convincingly that I'd expected.

"Alright, love, get in."

I don't need to be told twice. I jump in and give him the address, then sink back into the worn seats. The first thing I do is prise the ring on my keys apart and use it to take the battery out of my phone. I don't know much about technology, but I know that just turning it off isn't enough to stop it being tracked. Then I settle back and look out of the window, wondering what I'm about to walk into, and if it even matters – because really, what other option do I have? The driver tries to make conversation a few times, but eventually takes the hint and leaves me to my contemplation. I'm fighting exhaustion, I'm hungry, scared, alone, and every few minutes a shiver runs the length of my spine. But at least the headache has gone, and I can hear myself think.

It turns out that thinking is not my friend. My mind keeps returning to the basement, the cages, the racks and chains… it's everything I feared AbGen would be when I first set foot in Langford House, and worse. I'd gotten complacent. It was pure chance that I had one of Toby's pills in my pocket, otherwise I'd be locked in that basement right now, hobbled by Pearce's EM disruptor.

Oh, my God. This wasn't a spur of the moment, knee-jerk reaction to me wanting to leave. This had taken some serious planning: they'd developed the injection, tuned the disruptor, everything. They'd always planned to do this the moment I deviated from their script. I'd been Gardiner's property from the moment he sent Scott to track me down. My freedom was forfeit right from that very first shift.

"Are you alright, love?" The driver is eyeing me cautiously in the rear-view mirror, and I realise my breaths are coming in rapid bursts. I swallow and nod, and then force myself to take several long, slow breaths. I need to get a hold of myself. I still can't afford to fall apart. I have to keep it together until I'm safe. Whatever safe means for me now.

And then there's the girl. I can still see the dull resignation in her eyes, and I feel guilty as hell for leaving her behind, at Gardiner's mercy. I know there was nothing I could do to save her – I barely made it out of there myself – but that doesn't make it any easier knowing I abandoned her.

With my emotions tearing into me, the journey can't end soon enough, but eventually it does and then I wish it hadn't. Now I have to face Scott. Anxiety gripes at my stomach. I don't know if this is a trap or not, but there's only one way to find out. I hand the phone over to the driver, ignoring his half-hearted protests, and get out. The address I gave him is a few minutes away from the lake. When AbGen trace the phone – which they will – I want to make sure the driver can't tell them anything useful. Of course, that will be a moot point if I'm on my way to meet an agent who's still loyal to them.

As I trudge wearily along the dirt track, jumping at every sound, the birds are singing and crickets chirping, and the sun colours everything with its subtle rays, warming the air gently as it ripples through the long grass. It's far too beautiful a day for the world to come crashing down around me.

Then I look up and see him. Scott. He's sitting on the grassy bank, watching my approach wordlessly. He's wearing the same expression on his face as the first time we met, but he's clad in leathers instead of a suit. His helmet is on the ground next to him, and there's another one beside it.

I look around for the rest of them, because they've got to be waiting in ambush: this is a trap and he is the bait. As if reading my thoughts, he calls out softly,

"I've come alone."

He rises slowly to his feet, hands hanging loosely by his side. It reminds me of when I found him in standing my flat, trying not to spook me. Unbidden, the memory of his next visit to my flat flashes through my mind, with us curled up on the sofa together. I push it away angrily. I can't afford to think of him like that, not until I know for sure whether he was behind this.

He stoops to pick up the helmet and holds it out to me.

"Come on, we need to get moving. They could be here any moment."

"How do I know I can trust you?"

"We don't have time for this."

"Make time!"

"Look, you've already decided to trust me, or you wouldn't be here. And we need to move, now."

I back away, throwing a glance over my shoulder. Something isn't right here. I never should have come. If I go with him, I'll end up in that cage, I know it. I can't outrun him, but maybe I can shift. I've barely recovered from the last time, who knows where I'll end up or what state I'll be in… But it will buy me some time. I can't let them take me. I need to get out of here, I've got to–

"Anna, wait!"

"For what?" I demand, my anger undermined by the tremble in my voice. "For you to call Gardiner and claim your reward?"

"I'm not here for them."

I look into his eyes. I want to believe him so badly, to believe that there's someone – just one person – in this whole mess who's on my side. He holds his arms out to the side, showing me his hands, the same as that first time in my flat.

"Anna, if you want to run, I can't stop you. And I know I'll never find you again. But they will, and they won't stop looking until they do. You know how to run, but you don't know how to hide. Please, let me help you."

He holds the helmet out to me again, and I stare at his outstretched hand, weighing my options, running his words through my head. I search his face, my racing heart betraying my desperate desire to accept his words. I hesitate a moment longer, then reach out and take the helmet from him.

"Thank you," he breathes.

As I pull it down over my head, he shoulders a large backpack, then pulls his own helmet on and swings a leg over his bike. Actually, that's not his bike. I haven't seen this one before.

"Where's your Bandit?" I ask him, climbing onto the inferior machine.

"We can't risk using our own vehicles. They'll be tracking them."

"So where did this one come from?" I say, as he kicks it into life on the third attempt.

"I, uh, borrowed it."

I hope whoever he 'borrowed' it from doesn't notice it's gone missing for a while. We don't need the police on our tail on top of everything else. I don't plan on trading one cage for another. Scott twists the throttle and glances back over his shoulder.

"Hold on."

*

I do exactly that, wrapping my arms around him as we rattle down the dirt track then scream off to join the crush of traffic heading for the motorway. Scott rides like a man possessed, weaving in and out of vehicles, the whole time checking his mirrors and over his shoulder. I don't know if he's looking for cops or his former (at least, I hope former) colleagues, but eventually he seems to decide that we're clear and slows the bike to a less deadly speed. Blending in seems to be his main priority now, and he filters through the traffic only when necessary to avoid drawing attention to us.

I've lost track of how long we've been riding, but I'm shivering by the time we stop. I climb from the bike on unsteady legs and look around. We're in a poorly lit underground car park, with only three cars parked around us. One of them has been burnt out. The back of my neck tingles. If Scott thinks I'm hiding out here, he can think again. I turn around to tell him so, but as my eyes meet his, the words die in my throat. He's watching me with that expression again, the one that's both protective and uncertain, as intensely as he did that day in the canteen. Was all of that a lie, too?

I turn away awkwardly and reach for the chin strap on my helmet. My numb fingers fumble with the quick release, and he reaches under my chin and does it for me, leaving a tingle where his hands touch my skin.

"Sorry. There wasn't time to pick up your gloves."

My hands are trembling, but not from the cold. I thrust them into my pockets and thrust the unwanted thoughts away while I'm doing it. Scott – normally so good at reading me – seems oblivious. Small mercies.

"Come on, this way. Leave your lid," he adds. "We won't be needing it."

I put my helmet on the floor next to his. I doubt they'll still be here by the time we get back, but I'm starting to get the feeling we're not coming back – one way or the other.

As we emerge into the street, he pulls a hoodie from his backpack and passes it to me.

"Put this on – there are too many cameras around here."

I swallow. AbGen has access to CCTV feeds across the country. Of course. When am I going to stop being surprised by their reach? Scott pulls his hood up over his head, and I follow suit. And just like that, we're two anonymous hoods in...

"Where are we?"

"Birmingham." He glances up and down a street before leading me out onto it.

Birmingham. We're a long way from home. A long way from AbGen too, the optimist in me points out. Yeah, a long way from AbGen – but I sneak a glance at Scott and wonder how far from them I really am.

"This way," he says, interrupting my internal debate. I look up at the sign on the towering building in front of me. Birmingham International Rail Station. Surely this can't be a good idea, there are so many people...

Scott senses my hesitation.

"Crowds are a good thing. Trust me."

Like it's that easy. I doubt I'm going to be trusting anyone any time soon. But I guess there's some sense in what he's saying. We can blend in with a crowd, and from here we can get to anywhere in the country. It might buy us some time, at least. We stop at the departures board and he scans it for a moment.

"We've got some time. Let's grab some food while we can."

We settle at a sticky table in the middle of the busy food court with our overpriced junk food a few minutes later. Given that the only thing I've eaten since this morning is a chocolate bar, I should be starving, but I couldn't be less interested in food. My stomach's doing backflips and I can't summon the energy, or the inclination, to chew. I set the burger aside and wrap my hands around my coffee cup.

"You should eat."

I shake my head mutely and he doesn't press it. There's a sachet of sugar next to my cup, so I tear it open and pour it into my coffee, spilling half of the granules on the table top in the process. With a sigh, I abandon the coffee – I'm not really thirsty, anyway – and absentmindedly trace patterns in the spilled sugar.

Scott reaches out to put his hand over mine, and I pull away.

"I saw you," I blurt out. "When I was in Gardiner's office." It's neither a question nor an accusation, but a statement. Scott pulls his hand back with a nod, like he'd been expecting it.

"When you didn't come to the canteen, I was worried. Helen told me she saw you heading for Gardiner's office. I came looking for you, I wanted to make sure you didn't get into any trouble." He raises his hands defensively before I can accuse him of knowing more than he let on. "Not that sort of trouble. I thought you were going to get into an argument with him. I suppose I wasn't wrong about that part."

He falls silent for a moment, his face a mirror of what mine must have been when my world came crashing down.

"I'm sorry, Anna. You were right about him. I should have listened to you. But I–" He breaks off and stares out across the sea of faces rushing around us. Part of me wants to comfort him – it can't be easy confronting the truth about the man he's idolised for the last seven years.

The other part of me thinks I should take off while he's distracted.

"I never thought he was capable of something like this. When I saw him dragging you away, drugged…"

He looks back at me.

"I should have stopped him taking you, but I froze. It was unforgivable."

I close my eyes. I can't bear to see him beating himself up like this. Unforgivable? Maybe. It was no worse than what I'd done, though, shifting out and leaving that girl behind. It's time to stop with the half measures and holding other people to standards I can't meet myself. I need to trust Scott or lose my mind. I open my eyes and find him watching me intently. I hold his brilliant blue eyes for a long moment, watching our entire history play out across their surface. I know what I choose.

"It doesn't matter. You found me, that's all that counts. Just promise you won't leave me again."

"I swear it."

Chapter Seventeen

I tug my hood a little further forward over my face and keep my head down as I shuffle towards the front of the queue. A CCTV camera is directly above the booth and pointing at each customer as they are served. I tell myself not to stare at it, but my eyes keep darting towards the lens. A shiver runs down my spine. Is someone from AbGen watching me right now? I cough, my throat suddenly dry, and shuffle forwards again.

The man inside the booth scowls at me – my fashion statement isn't winning me any friends – and I clear my throat.

"Two singles to Leeds, please."

"A hundred and twenty-three pounds."

I hand over the cash Scott has given me and his scowl deepens, but after a moment he slides the tickets to me and I scoop them up and hurry away, my heart pounding.

Scott is waiting for me by the departures board, and my gaze flickers over it.

"How long until our train leaves?" I ask, handing over the tickets.

"We're not going by train." He starts walking, and tosses the tickets in a bin.

"What? Why not?" I scurry along by his side, staring back at the bin.

"We're taking a plane to Belfast. I just booked us two tickets on my phone. This way."

I get on the escalator a step behind him.

"You paid by card?" I'm not an expert, but that seems like a bad idea. "Won't they be able to trace that?"

"Exactly. They'll assume it's a decoy. I've bought tickets to Berlin as well, just in case. It should buy us a little time to disappear."

Oh. Makes sense, I suppose. I'm glad Scott's on my side. He was right: I have no idea how to run from AbGen.

We hurry through the building, keeping our hoods up and sticking with the crowds. We make it onto the plane with just a few minutes to spare, and I'm glad there won't be too much waiting around in front of the cameras. My nerves are wound so tight that I don't think I could stomach the sitting around.

As we claim our seats, I wonder how I'm going to pass the next hour of doing exactly that, but it turns out I needn't have worried. As soon as I sink into the seat the exhaustion catches up with me. I close my eyes just for a moment, and the next thing I know a hand is shaking my shoulder. I start, my eyes flying open.

"Easy." Scott withdraws his hand. "We're here."

I blink rapidly and wait for my heart rate to slow. The steady stream of people passing our seats slows and we ease out and work our way through arrivals. We have no luggage to collect, so we're on our way quickly. Scott hails a taxi and gives the driver an address as we climb into the back.

"We've got a while. Get some more sleep if you want," Scott says as the car pulls away, and my eyes are closed before he finishes speaking.

I jolt awake again when the car comes to a stop and look around.

"Where are we?"

"Ulster. We're making a pit stop."

He passes some money to the driver, tells him to keep the change, and we step out onto the street. In front of us is a large, modern building with elegant glass fronting. Above, golden lettering reads 'Ulster Investment Society'. I look to Scott, but he's already pushing the glass doors open and stepping inside. I hurry after him as he strides to the counter, looking around me and feeling distinctly out of place in this upper-class bank. I'm practically a zombie after Pearce's super insulin shot, my clothes are a mess after sleeping on the plane and in the cab, and my hair bears an uncanny resemblance to a bird's nest. Around me, people are dressed in suits and ties, immaculately clean and wearing professional smiles.

If the woman behind the counter has an opinion on my appearance, no hint of it reaches her face, which is

216

framed by glossy blonde locks and highlighted by the merest traces of makeup.

"Good afternoon, sir. How may I help you today?" she asks, with a lilting Irish accent that reminds me I'm no longer in my home country. A wave of sadness passes over me. Will we go ever go back there, or is our future in Ireland, or France, or some place halfway round the world? I moved around too much as a kid to ever put down roots, but over the last few years I'd come to think of Whitelyn as home. Sure, it's no idyllic English village, and my flat no quaint cottage, but it was mine, and it was the first time I'd been able to say that.

My melancholy goes unnoticed by Scott, who slides an ID card across the counter.

"I'd like to access my safe deposit box, please."

She picks up the ID card and checks the name on it.

"Certainly, Mr Harrison. Right this way, please."

We follow her through the bank and past its many workers at a brisk pace, and she unlocks a door, and then withdraws discretely with all the professionalism I'd expect from someone who looks like her and works somewhere like this. I turn three-sixty, looking around at the row upon row of boxes. I can't even imagine how much wealth is concealed in this room; there's no saying what any of those boxes might contain. I've never seen one up close before – it's not like I've ever had the need, given that my savings have rarely exceeded three figures, and the only thing of any real value I'd ever possessed was the ring that started all this. And, frankly, the less said about that, the better. In truth, I'm a little disappointed. Aside from the nondescript grey boxes, there's a table and two chairs in the room, and not much else. I'd imagined it all to be a little more…. I don't know, just *more*.

Scott pulls his box from the wall and inserts his key. It's a small box, maybe ten inches by fifteen, and I'd like to know what could be in there that's so important we had to come all the way to Northern Ireland to get it. The lid swings open and my question is answered. Nestled inside the box are half a dozen stacks of bank notes – various currencies – and what look to be several passports and driving licences. Lying in the middle of the box is a black handgun with two spare magazines. The weapon draws my eye: a Glock, I recognise from my training back at AbGen. Scott picks it up, checks the chamber, ejects the magazine, then places it into the backpack along with the two spare clips. He shuffles through the passports and selects one, and then looks through the driving licences, presumably for one that matches. As he removes some of the stacks of money, a thought strikes me, and I sit on one of the chairs, vaguely aware they probably cost more than my flat, turning it over in my mind.

"You said you trusted Gardiner." Again and again he told me he trusted the man, but his little stash here somewhat suggests otherwise. He stops what he's doing and looks at me.

"I did. Anna, I trusted the man with my life. Why wouldn't I?"

He dumps the backpack on the table, and perches on its edge, his shoulders slumped. I feel a stab of guilt for my accusation. Hard as this has been for me, I can only imagine what he's going through. He gave Gardiner seven years of his life; a life that he almost threw away because of his talent.

"I never thought I would use any of this stuff. I set it up because Gardiner told me to."

That sets alarm bells ringing and I'm up out of my seat before my brain has caught up with my mouth.

"He knows about this?"

Scott shakes his head.

"No. He told all of us to set up a bolt-box, in case anything ever happened to AbGen and we had to go to ground. He also told us to keep their locations to ourselves, so that if he was compromised he could never give us up."

And there I go again, leaping to conclusions like it's an Olympic sport. Meanwhile, Scott looks like a drowning man who just watched the last life raft disappear into the horizon.

"I'm sorry," I tell him, breaking away from his gaze. Sorry for my accusations, sorry for dragging him into this mess, sorry for ruining everything he's built in the last seven years.

"Hey. You have nothing to be sorry for." He hooks a finger under my chin and turns my face back to him. "Nothing, you hear me?"

I close the gap between us and press my lips to his. He tenses and I freeze. Shit. Have I just made a huge mistake? I have. He doesn't see me that way. I should have known he would never look at me like that, he–

He's wrapping an arm around me, drawing me closer still, his lips coming to life against mine. I press my body against his, reaching up into the kiss as he leans down, my eyelids closing as I give myself over to him…

And suddenly he's gone. My eyes fly open and he's standing a pace away, his shoulders rigid as he stares at the door.

"What's wrong?" I ask, scanning for danger. My heart is pounding, from the kiss, from the fear, I don't know which.

"Someone's coming. One of them."

I don't need to ask who he means. There's only one question to ask, and I ask it as he tosses the remaining money from the safe box into the backpack.

"How long?"

"They're within a mile. I'm sorry. I should have sensed them coming."

As if anyone has to apologise to me of all people for not having perfect control of their talent. I take hold of his hand.

"Come on, let's go."

He nods, scoops up the bag, and we take a deep breath before leaving the room. We can't afford to draw attention to ourselves. Anything that raises suspicion could draw AbGen down on top of us. They're close, but we're not caught yet. We can still get out of here without leaving a trail.

We leave the bank in strained silence, broken only when Scott thanks the cashier and flashes her a confident smile. I hope it doesn't look as forced to her as it does to me. We get outside and the cool air brushes the back of my neck, sending a shudder through me. My skin is clammy and I can feel a sweat breaking out on my forehead. I'm not going back. I'm never going back.

"Breathe, Anna," Scott tells me, and I see the concern on his face. I nod, and swallow the urge to asking him if they're getting closer. It doesn't matter either way – we're not sticking around to wait for them. Scott flags down a taxi and we're on our way again.

Our driver takes one look at the wad of cash Scott offers him and doesn't ask questions. Smart man. From the focus on Scott's face, I figure he must be keeping tabs on the agents' location and directing the driver in the opposite direction to them. That's what I'd do, if I had a talent that was actually useful, rather than a giant pain in my arse. After about twenty minutes his face relaxes and he leans back in the seat until Ulster is a distant memory in our rear-view mirror.

We pass an anxious night in a quiet bed-and-breakfast on the outskirts of some anonymous town whose name I don't even bother to register. We're not going to be here long. Scott books a twin room, separate beds, and pays with cash. Both of us are too tired to talk about what happened back in the bank, but somehow I end up curled up against him as we fall asleep.

When I wake, I'm alone in the bed, and lie there silently for a moment, running yesterday's events through my mind. Now is still not the time to break down, but that's okay. I can hear Scott in the shower room, reminding me I'm not alone anymore. Maybe, just maybe, we can get through this. Together. With his experience and his talent, and my… I dunno, I'm sure I bring something to the table. Paranoia, maybe?

Just then, Scott comes out of the bathroom with his hair still damp and flashes me a smile. I return it with a slight blush, not meeting his eye, and slip past him. I find the hotel toiletries on the edge of the sink and make use of them before getting into the shower. As the water cascades around me, sending a disconcerting amount of grime down the drain, I think over the thing – the face – that's been bothering me all night. There are some tough decisions to be made.

I emerge some time later with a towel wrapped around my hair, and my mind set. Scott has ordered room service – exactly how long was I in the shower for? – and the smell is enough to drive everything else from my head. He hands me a mug of coffee. I blow across the surface and take a sip, then start in on the food. We eat in silence for a moment, then I broach the subject that's been on my mind.

"We need to talk about yesterday. When you saw me in the office–"

He looks like he's about to apologise again, so I raise a hand to stop him. Hard as it is to do, I need to go back to where it started, so he understands what I'm saying.

"You told me you froze. I get it. You're not the only one who's done things they're not proud of."

I tell him all of it – Gardiner wanting to weaponise me, the injection, the basement. The girl. Once the words start tumbling out of me, I don't seem able to stop them. Scott doesn't interrupt, he just lets me get it all out, but as I reach the part about the cages, he grips the table top until his knuckles turn white.

"So we can't just run," I tell him. "We have to find a way to save her, and anyone else they're planning on locking up in there. She's an absa, she's got to be. That could have been me, or you, or anyone else we care about. We've got to stop them."

"Anna… You know what this means, right? If we go back there, there's no guarantee either of us will walk away."

"We have to try."

He runs his hand over his face, and then nods.

"You're right. Any ideas how we're going to get back in there?"

"Yeah. Through the front door."

C. S. CHURTON

Chapter Eighteen

Good morning, Scott. I must say you certainly have a talent for doing the unexpected." Gardiner's voice filters into the car, distorted by the phone's speaker. "I confess I rather thought my secretary was joking when she told me you were on the line. I take it you're with the lovely Anna?"

"I am," Scott says.

"Good morning, Anna." He's suspiciously upbeat, as if he was greeting a colleague as opposed to speaking to the people he's spent days hunting across two countries.

"I'm afraid she's not up to talking right now."

"Oh?"

I can hear Gardiner working to keep his voice nonchalant, but he's not quite pulling it off. Or maybe I'm just imagining it. My heart is hammering in my chest and making it hard to follow the conversation.

"I've given her an insulin shot."

"I see. And why would you do that?"

Scott exhales heavily.

"I know you think I've gone rogue, but it was the only way I could get Anna to trust me. I thought I could convince her to come back in willingly. It didn't work, so I had to take more decisive action."

"You've invested an awful lot of energy in giving us the run-around, so you'll forgive me if I'm a little cynical about your sudden change of loyalties."

"My loyalty has always been to AbGen," Scott replies fiercely, his hands clenching around the steering wheel. "I couldn't call in a sit-rep, Anna was suspicious enough of me as it was. If she'd shifted again, we'd never have found her. This was our best shot – she's always listened to me before."

"But not this time?" Gardiner has recovered his poise and his voice is calm again.

"No. Not this time. She was too spooked. She wouldn't listen to reason."

"And exactly how much has Anna told you?"

"About the basement? Everything." Scott sighs again. Apparently my habits have rubbed off on him. "I'm not going to lie, boss, I'm disappointed you didn't tell me. I thought you trusted me. But I can understand your reasons."

"Interesting. Your psychological profile suggested you would have found the idea… challenging."

"Then you need better profilers. I care about Anna, but I love our country. I can't justify putting one girl's freedom above the lives of the entire population. I won't."

I shoot Scott a look. He said that with entirely too much conviction, but I suppose he's got to be convincing if our plan's going to work. We're only getting one shot at this, and they're probably already tracing the call. He smiles at me reassuringly. I bite my lower lip and turn back to the phone resting on the dash.

"I agree. It's just a pity young Anna doesn't feel the same way, but I'm sure we can persuade her. How do you propose we proceed?"

"I'm driving to you now. Our ETA is in about an hour. I'll stay with you until she's secure in the basement and then I'm at your disposal. Oh, and Isaac? If I'm bringing a drugged-up girl in through the front door, you might want to make sure the mind reader's on a break."

*

The closer we get to AbGen, the worse my anxiety gets. We spent all of yesterday and half of last night going over our plan, but Scott goes through it with me again – either he thinks I have a memory impairment or he's just as on edge as I am. The plan itself is simple: with Gardiner convinced I'm drugged and Scott's loyal to AbGen, we can walk straight in through the front door. We can't risk running into Joe because he'd see through our ruse right away. There's a reason AbGen puts a mind reader on the door. But Gardiner has just as much reason for preventing that meeting as we do, so Scott is confident our path will be clear.

Once inside, Gardiner will want us in his office and away from prying eyes – which is exactly where we want to be. From there, I'll shift directly downwards and into the basement – Scott isn't a fan of this part of the plan; he thinks it puts me in harm's way. But I refuse to be sidelined and let him take all the risk. My EM pulse will knock out the base's power, including the EM disruptor, and the locks on the cages, allowing me to get the girl out, and video the basement using a concealed camera. I've promised Scott that if anything goes wrong, I'll shift again and get well clear of Langford House, but there's no way I'm leaving him alone. And his job is far more dangerous than mine – while I'm groping around in the dark, in the last place anyone expects me to be, he'll be making sure our escape route through the office stays clear. Hopefully, everyone will start sweeping the base for me, but if not… He tried to reassure me last night by reminding me he's carrying a gun. This is the part of the plan I'm not a fan of, because as I pointed out last night, he won't be the only one with a gun.

If we make it that far – and Scott is overwhelmingly confident that we will – then we simply take advantage of the confusion to get out. Gardiner can't issue a directive to stop us leaving the base, not without risking a mutiny when the rest of AbGen's agents learn that he's holding people against their will.

We've run out of scenarios to talk through by the time the car comes to a stop. I pull a sugar pill from my pocket and it feels like paper mache when I put it in my mouth. It's one thing planning this, but now that Langford House is looming above me, it's suddenly very real, and the enormity of our task is pressing down on me. We should have just kept running.

Scott leans over to squeeze my shoulder. I try to arrange my face into something resembling a smile and nod at him. He nods back.

"Okay, let's do this."

I chew the pill as he gets out of the car and walks round to my side, opening my door and helping me out. I let him assist me – it's possible we're already being watched – and try to focus on how I felt when Gardiner drugged me. I let my feet stumble up the curb and lean heavily into Scott. From his grunt, I assume I'm doing a convincing job. He wraps an arm around my shoulder and steers me to AbGen's door.

"Is the street secure?" a voice queries through the speaker.

"There's a party across the road," Scott replies, his voice calm and steady and a complete contrast to my rapid heartbeat and ragged breathing. I stare down at my feet and force myself to bring it under control. I'm supposed to be out of it, not acutely aware that I'm about to walk into the lion's den, where if things go wrong I'll be locked in a cage in dark, at the mercy of a man who's already proved he has no limits on how far he'll go and–

Scott's hand tightens momentarily on my shoulder and I take a steadying breath. It's going to be fine. He won't let anything happen to me.

I keep my eyes on my feet as we cross the threshold and the door clicks shut behind us.

"Follow me, please," a voice instructs us in clipped tones. I don't recognise it: good news for us. Joe's natural curiosity would have blown our cover for sure.

We're moving forward again and I let my eyes slide over the carpet as we go. I don't trust myself to look around, certain my expression will betray my terror. We step into the lift and the door slides shut, trapping us inside with the agent.

The lift rumbles into life, hauling us closer to Gardiner. A shudder runs through me and my stomach starts to gnaw at itself. There are so many ways this could go wrong. What if I can't shift when I'm supposed to? What if I end up in one of those cages? What am I doing here? This is crazy, I'm crazy, I should never have come back here. I need to get out, I've got to get away, I've got to–

I've got to *stay*. I swallow the lump in my throat. It's not just me anymore. I can't leave Scott to face them on his own. I've got to see this through.

The lift jerks to a halt and the doors slide open. A hand takes my arm – whose, I don't know, and I don't dare look – and steers me through it, along the corridor until we're standing in front of the imposing dark oak door. Our escort raises a hand and raps once on the wood.

"Come," Gardiner's voice instructs from within, and I jump at the sound of it. I need to do better than this. *Get a grip, Anna.* Of course he's inside – he's hardly likely to have popped out for a cup of tea.

The guard opens the door and ushers us inside. Scott steers me over the threshold while I lean into him and try to make my movements slow and uncoordinated. I hope to hell I can fool someone who's already seen me drugged. I force myself to lift my head a fraction and look around unsteadily, as though I'm having trouble focussing. Gardiner is seated behind his extravagant desk, looking a little too smug, but his reptilian eyes are hard as they slide over the pair of us. Walter Pearce is standing at his right shoulder, his innocent façade so completely at odds with what he did to me last time I was in this office that I could almost imagine he was innocent of it. Almost. My mouth goes dry as I recall the way his poison felt as it flooded through me, and suddenly I'm not worried about not being able to shift anymore. Now I'm worried I won't be able to stop myself from shifting too early.

The door clicks shut behind us, though I can't tell if the guard is inside the office or in the corridor. Either way, it's too late to back out now. We're committed.

"It would seem we have a lot to talk about," Gardiner says, tearing his eyes from me and fixing them on Scott. I feel Scott stiffen to attention beside me, as much as he's able to with one arm wrapped around my waist.

"Yes, sir. I would have kept you informed, had I been able," Scott tells him, his voice contrite.

"No matter, you're here now," Gardiner replies, and I get the sense anything is forgivable of the man who's brought the boss's favourite toy home. I barely suppress a shudder. A polite cough sounds from Pearce's direction, and Gardiner smiles apologetically at Scott.

"Walter is right, of course; this conversation can wait until after we get Anna settled into her new accommodation."

If he's looking for a reaction from Scott, then he's going to be disappointed. My acting skills may be a little sketchy, but if there's one thing I've learned on my travels with Scott, it's that if he ever takes up poker as a career, Vegas would be in trouble. I'm still leaning against him and he doesn't so much as twitch. He does, however, move the hand that's 'supporting' me ever so slightly, pressing the heel of his palm into my side.

It's the signal. He's right. If they get me into the basement before I knock out the disruptor then it's all over.

I can hear him talking, but I shut out the noise and focus on the fear locked away inside of me, letting it rise to the surface. A nagging voice reminds me I've never managed to control where I end up before, tells me I'm going to blow it, and leave Scott stranded here alone, adding to the overwhelming terror coursing through me. Then, against every instinct telling me to get the hell away from this place, I picture the basement in my mind. I have to get out of here. I need to get into the basement. I've got to get down there, I've got to–

*

I raise a hand to steady myself, and touch something cold and metallic. I jerk my hand away and open my eyes. Darkness.

"Where... where did you come from?" a tremulous voice asks from nearby. I turn towards its source, my eyes picking out a small figure as they adjust to the gloom. I'm definitely in the right place. Bars separate me from the figure curled up in the corner of a cell. I recognise the scrawny figure and dirty-blonde hair of the girl I saw before, with no small amount of relief.

"It's okay, I'm here to help you," I promise in a hoarse whisper.

"No. No, it's a trick, it's a trap," she wails, her voice rising in hysteria. She starts to rock frantically. I look around in alarm. No one's coming. It's me she's afraid of.

"Shh, shh, it's okay," I promise, slowly crouching down and showing her my hands, even though she's steadfastly refusing to look at me. What the hell have they done to her? "I'm not going to make you go anywhere."

She carries on whimpering as though I hadn't spoken, and I curse inwardly. Why did I just assume she would come with me? I should have seen this coming. She's probably been locked up in here for months, no wonder she's terrified of leaving. Looking more closely, I can see her clothes are little more than rags – her shirt has a button missing and her black jeans are ripped at the bottom of one leg, and her shoes are old and dirty. Her face is streaked with dirt. It makes it hard to tell her age, but she can't be any older than me. There but for the grace of God...

I shake the thought away and push myself up from the floor; she shows no reaction. If we're going to get out of here, I can't afford to hang around. My EM pulse has taken the power offline, leaving the cages unlocked, but there's no telling how quickly the backup generators will kick in. We can deal with the psychological damage later –

right now I need to focus on getting the evidence and getting us both out of here. I pull a shoe off and wedge it in her cell door before it can relock itself, then grope for the chain around my neck, slipping it out from under my t-shirt. The charm on it – courtesy of Scott's Ulster contact – looks like something you'd pick up at any marketplace, but set in the centre is a small camera. He assures me it will work even in the dark. I feel for the tiny button on the back and press it, hoping it's had time to recover from the pulse. I hurry around the room, pausing briefly by each cage and piece of equipment, letting the camera do its thing. I finish up outside the occupied cage, letting the camera get a good look at the imprisoned girl.

A whirring starts up. We're running out of time. The power will be back on any moment.

"Hey," I say softly to the girl, working against the adrenaline pounding in my ears. "My name's Anna, what's yours?"

She doesn't reply, but turns her head slowly towards me. For a moment I see what I think is pure hatred in her eyes, but when I blink it's gone – if it was ever there at all – and her eyes are dull with vacant resignation.

"I don't know how long you've been down here, or what they've told you, but don't you want to see your family and your friends again? I bet they've missed you. I can take you to them. All you have to do is come with me."

I stretch my hand out to her and wait, barely daring to draw breath. If this doesn't work, then all of this has been for nothing. The thought strikes me like a physical blow. We risked everything. Scott put his life on the line for me. I can't let it be for nothing.

"Come with me and he'll never touch you again, I promise."

Slowly, her hand reaches out towards me, inching closer. A jolt of electricity sparks between us as her fingertips reach mine, then I wrap my hand around hers and pull her to her feet. She squeezes my hand, digging her fingernails into my flesh. I gasp in pain.

"Hey, it's okay," I whisper. "It's okay."

Static tingles across my hand as she stares at me, vulnerability plastered all over her face, and maybe it makes me a bad person, but all I can think is we can't afford to do this right now. Not yet. We need to get out of here before we're both locked in a cage.

A loud buzz comes from across the room. We both jump, and I spin towards it, gripping the hand in mine to keep myself anchored in the room. I can't shift and leave her here alone. My scattered energy makes my head swim, but I force my eyes to focus as the lift door slides open and a silhouette pauses on the threshold. The light behind it burns my retinas, but not so badly that I can't see the gun raised and sweeping the room in time with the figure's head. It turns towards us, the gun levelling at us, and I force my eyes away from it and onto the figure's face…

Scott. It's Scott. Relief washes over me, leaving me swaying on my feet. My hand hangs limply in the prisoner's grip and I can feel her nails digging into me.

"It's okay," I tell her, finding my voice at last. "He's with us."

Scott hurries towards us, lowering the weapon as he crosses the floor.

"Anna, thank God," he says, his relief a mirror of my own. "You were gone so long I thought you'd run into trouble."

"We're fine," I tell him with a conviction I don't quite feel. At this, his eyes leave my face for the first time, and fall on the shape beside me. A frown crosses his features.

"Megan?"

"Wait, you know her?"

I don't know why I'm shocked, it makes perfect sense that he'd have met her before Gardiner decided to lock her away for lacking patriotic spirit.

"I recruited her. They told me she turned down Gardiner's job offer. That was months ago. They–" He breaks off as the full horror of it hits him.

"We can do this later. We've got to go."

He nods, his jaw set in grim determination.

"Stay behind me."

He raises his weapon again and starts moving back towards the staircase. I follow him, towing Megan behind me. As we pass through the cell door, I pause to yank my shoe back on, then hurry after him. The door clangs shut, and a loud bleep tells me it's locked again. I don't have time to dwell on how close I came to being on the wrong side of the door, which is probably for the best. We step inside the lift and Scott turns to me as it rumbles to life.

"The office was empty when I left – they're all searching for you – but we may have to fight our way out of here. If that happens, you've got to shift."

"No way, I–" I protest.

"Anna," he says, his voice cutting across mine and leaving no room for argument. "I can get me and Megan out of here, but I can't do it unless I know you're safe, and I can't protect all three of us. If anyone's in that office, you shift, you hear me?"

I nod unhappily. How can I argue when he puts it like that? My being here is putting him in danger. Again.

He reaches out and brushes his thumb against my cheek.

"Hey, we'll be together again soon."

He reaches in and touches his lips to mine, just briefly. The lift slows to a halt, leaving me no time to dwell. I can still feel the electricity of the kiss as he raises his weapon, and the door rolls open.

Chapter Nineteen

D rop the gun."

It's Gardiner, and he looks completely unperturbed by the turn of events. In front of him stand two armed guards. I recognise one of them as Marcus, the guard from the basement. My heart squeezes painfully. There was a reason he wasn't down there. The other is the one who escorted us into Gardiner's office. Both of them have their weapons drawn and trained on Scott.

Gardiner suspected all along. He'd just given us enough rope to hang ourselves.

"I won't ask you again."

"Anna, go," Scott tells me, without taking his eyes from the threat.

Panic flutters in my throat. Leaving him here alone is a death sentence, no matter what he said back in the lift – we both know I'm the one they want. *I'm the one they want.* The thought flashes through my mind like a lightning strike, illuminating everything for a fleeting moment. They want me, and there are no limits to what they'd do to keep me. They'd give up Scott to have me in a heartbeat. It's a good trade as far as I'm concerned. I just need to get out of here first.

I close my eyes and think of the guns pointing at us, the guns I have to get away from. I need to get out of here, I need to get to the lake, I've got to–

"Anna, get out of here!" Scott's urgent voice makes me jump, and my eyes fly open in surprise. A split second later, a scorching pain flashes through my skull. Why am I still here? That should have worked, maybe not have taken me right to the lake, but I shouldn't still be *here*.

Megan takes two quick steps backwards and suddenly there's a snarl on her face and a gun in her hands, and it's aiming at Scott.

"Shift and I'll kill him," she warns me. I stare at her, bewildered by her actions. Gone is the cowering girl from the basement: this Megan is confident, professional, and cold. Her body isn't weak and wasted, as I thought in the dim light of the basement. Her baggy clothing was hiding a lean frame covered in wiry muscles. Her eyes never leave me. Eyes that are brimming with the hatred I saw before.

"Now, now," Gardiner says from behind his bodyguards, his voice benign. "There's no need for that, Megan. Young Anna couldn't shift even if she wanted to – as I suspect she has already discovered."

His eyes rivet me to the spot, and off to my side I see Megan nod and lower the gun. How does he know I'm grounded – what the hell is going on here? He sighs like a parent disciplining a pair of naughty children and turns his attention to Scott.

"I'm disappointed in you, Scott. You used to be far more perceptive before you started spending time with Ms Mason. Did you really believe I would allow you to walk back in here without taking certain measures?"

He strolls to a cabinet – he's really revelling in his moment of glory – and opens it to reveal a black cylindrical device.

"I took the precaution of having Walter install an EM-shielded disruptor – it's been active from the moment you first shifted. Now, Scott, put your weapon down, before we're forced to take matters into our own hands."

Despair hits me like a physical force as Scott's shoulders hunch in defeat and he ejects the clip from the gun, then raises his hands for Megan to disarm him. Gardiner nods in satisfaction and Megan steps forward, closing her hand around the weapon. I stare at her with undisguised hatred. To think we threw away our freedom for her.

Scott swings an elbow into her face, catching both her and me off guard. Before I have time to even consider what I should do, she barrels at him, blood streaming from her nose, and lands a solid kick to his midriff. He staggers back and crashes into the solid oak desk, groping the edge for support – or, at least, that's what it looks like. His fingers, hidden from everyone else in the room, are edging closer to a button under the desk. I don't know what it does, but I know he's going to need a distraction while he finds it.

"Get away from him!" I scream, and throw myself at Megan, self-defence lessons forgotten. My punch sails past her face and she slams a fist into my stomach with contemptuous ease. I double over, winded and reeling from the force of her punch, and she levels her gun at me.

"Alright, alright!" Scott says, raising his hands and shooting me a look. Whatever he needed to do, it's done. I hope it was worth it. Jesus, Megan packs a punch. Wheezing, I mimic his gesture and show my empty palms.

"I hope we shall not have to endure any more ill-conceived escape attempts," Gardiner says. His voice is dripping with disapproval and he's looking at us both in distaste. Scott shakes his head.

"Good. There's no need for any harm to come to either of you."

I seethe silently at the blatant lie. I saw the machinery in his basement.

"I won't give you any more trouble. Just don't hurt Anna."

"How very gallant. You have my word. Daniel." He glances at one of his bodyguards. "Cuff him."

Daniel lowers his gun and produces a pair of handcuffs. Scott's face is a blank slate as the man advances on him warily and takes hold of his wrist. Resigned, Scott allows him to snap the cuff around it, and pull it behind his back, where it's locked to his other wrist. And just like that, the last trace of hope is gone. Daniel grunts in satisfaction and steps back.

Across the room, the office door slams inward, and we all spin round in alarm. Joe stands outlined in the doorway, weapon raised and sweeping amongst us. Gardiner looks from him to Scott and his eyes narrow. Realisation strikes me at the same moment.

"I heard the panic alarm," Joe says. Scott's plan was both brilliant and reckless: a proper Hail Mary. The question is, can we trust Joe, or does his loyalty to Gardiner run too deep?

"Thank you, Joe," Gardiner says. "We have everything in hand. Unfortunately, two of your former colleagues have gone dark, but I think we can handle it from here."

"Yes, sir," Joe says, eyeing the pair of us uneasily.

"He's lying," I tell Joe. "Listen to me." I run my mind over everything – Pearce injecting me, the basement, my escape. I show him me and Scott running, and our near misses with AbGen.

"No," Joe shakes his head. "You're lying. You think I can't tell the difference?"

"Then listen to him," Scott says. "Tell him, Gardiner. Tell him about your little prison cells."

A shadow passes behind Gardiner's eyes as he works to keep his face impassive, but it's not his face Joe is reading.

"Tell him about how you like to torture girls in the name of patriotic duty," Scott demands. "Tell him that everything he's worked for is a lie."

"Enough!" Joe snaps, stalking across the room. He raises his gun and smashes it down into Scott's face.

"No!" I scream as Scott hits the ground, launching myself forwards – to do what, I don't know.

"Anna, don't," Scott grunts.

I stop, looking to him uncertainly. He's mouthing something at me. I can't make it out. Can't? Keep? Key!

Key? What does that mean? And then I see it: the small silver object that he's curled around. Joe gave him a key; he's on our side. But he can't use it with everyone watching him.

"Please," I say, taking a step toward Gardiner, and every gun in the room follows me. "Don't hurt him, I'll do whatever you want, I promise. Just let him go."

"Very touching, Anna. But I think we're beyond that now. Daniel, please take Scott downstairs. I don't think we require his presence at the moment."

The guard reaches down to pull Scott to his feet and my heart pounds frantically. I can only hope he had enough time to use the key. If they put him in the basement, neither of us is ever getting out of here.

It happens so quickly that his movements are a blur – one moment Daniel is towering over him, the next the guard is on the floor, writhing in pain. The sound of the gunshot doesn't reach my ears right away, and when it does, Scott is already on his feet, swinging the smoking gun to target the other bodyguard, cuffs hanging from one wrist.

Behind him, Megan lifts her gun and I throw myself at her. We collide with a solid thud that knocks the breath out of us both, and then we're on the floor, grappling for the weapon. She's stronger than me; there's no way I can wrestle it from her hands. My self-defence classes belatedly come flooding back to me, and I swing my elbow into her face, and again. I feel something crunch – her or me, I don't know. I draw my fist back and hit her again, and this time I can't hear anything above the pounding in my ears. My fury at all the betrayals – hers, Pearce's, Gardiner's – breaks through to the surface and I

246

keep swinging. She was going to kill him. She's *not* going to kill him.

"Anna! Anna, stop!" Scott's shouts break through and I freeze mid-swing, staring at my bloodied hand as the red mist fades, and then beyond to Megan's unconscious form.

"Are you okay?"

I nod shakily and look around. Joe is guarding the door, Gardiner is watching us warily, and Daniel is deathly still. The other guard, Marcus, is on his knees, with his hands interlocked behind his head and gun discarded on the floor beside him. I can't bring myself to feel sorry for either of them. They would happily have chucked me in that cage under Gardiner's orders.

I snatch up Megan's gun and get to my feet.

"What now?"

"Now we're leaving."

He keeps his gun on the kneeling guard and advances on him.

"Take it easy," the man says, eyeing Scott warily. "I was just following orders."

Scott removes the remaining cuff from his wrist in stony silence, apparently as unimpressed by that defence as I am. He wastes no time snapping the cuff around the man's wrist. The guard twists suddenly, sweeping out with a leg and sending Scott crashing to the floor before I can even utter a warning. Marcus is on him in a flash, grabbing his gun hand and slamming it repeatedly into the floor again and again. The gun flies across the room, and the guard lifts his boot and smashes it down onto Scott's hand. The bones break with a sickening crunch that seems to echo around the room. I stare at the heavy metal weapon in my hands and start to lift it, but then Scott is on his feet, his right hand hanging limp by his side, slamming his forehead into the guard's face. The man crumples to the floor and goes still. Whether he's unconscious or just dazed, I don't know.

I see movement out of the corner of my eye and turn on my heel. The gun comes with me and I find myself pointing it at Gardiner. He freezes, and the room falls utterly silent. Even Gardiner has no words.

"Do it," Scott says quietly. "It's the only way you'll ever be free."

He's right. I can pull the trigger right now and end all of it. Or we can spend the rest of our lives running. More people will be locked away and tortured. Gardiner will keep corrupting absas. It's the right choice. The only choice. My finger doesn't move. My vision blurs and I'm angrily blinking back tears and my finger still doesn't move. I shake my head and my hands tremble. A sob of frustration escapes from my throat. I'll never be free.

A shot rings out and I jump, staring at my gun in horror. No, it wasn't mine. My finger is still wrapped loosely around the trigger. Even as Gardiner slides to the floor I look across at Joe and see the telltale wisp of smoke leaking from his barrel.

"Now you're free," he says, lowering the weapon.

A hand closes around my gun and I jump. Scott's. It's Scott's hand. Gently he pushes down on the weapon with his left hand until it's pointing at the floor ground. His right hand is still hanging uselessly beside him. He says nothing to me but looks at our saviour.

"You need to get out of here."

"I think that's my line," Joe says, with the ghost of a smile.

"You think he's going to let me take the fall for this?" Scott says with a meaningful nod at the downed guard, who's watching the exchange in silence. "Get your family and go. I'm sorry we dragged you into this."

Joe shakes his head, his lips pressed together in a stubborn line.

"Not everyone here is corrupt. I have to stay. I'm the only one who can weed out the rest of them. Get her out of here. I'll make sure you don't have to run forever." He makes eye contact with me as he says this last part, and I nod, unable to speak. "Get out of here. Find the Ishmaelians."

Scott clasps him on the shoulder.

"Thank you."

He picks up his dropped weapon, though I've got no idea if he can fire it left-handed.

"Come on, Anna," he says, stepping through the open door. I take one last look around the room, at the unconscious girl we came to rescue, the sullen but wisely passive guard, and the two dead bodies, then step through after him.

Chapter Twenty

I stick close behind Scott as he hurries along the hallway, awkwardly tucking his weapon into his waistband as he goes. That seems like a really dumb idea to me, and I keep mine in my sweating hand for three more steps before he glances back over his shoulder at me.

"We need to blend in. No one knows what's happened yet, and anyone walking around with a loaded weapon is going to stand out like a sore thumb."

He nods to the gun and I reluctantly concede that he has a point. Discretion is our best weapon now. I slip the handgun into my waistband against the small of my back and pull my top down to cover it. We get moving again and Scott hides his hand in his clothing. I guess injuries are a dead giveaway, too.

"Does it hurt?" I ask, and then feel like the biggest idiot in the whole building – and I've got some stiff competition. Of course it hurts. I heard the bones breaking.

"It's fine," he says, jabbing the call button on the lift with his left hand. I arch a brow at the blatant lie, and he amends with a shrug, "It's the least of our problems right now."

Now that I can't argue with. The lift doors slide open and we step inside. My foot taps an impatient rhythm on the metallic floor as the doors close again. It might be the fastest way out of here, but standing still while adrenaline is pounding in my ears is hell. What if someone's worked out what's happening? What if the guard overpowered Joe? What if–

A hand touches my arm, and I meet Scott's eye.

"It's going to be okay," he says. "I'm going to get you out of here."

I nod and swallow the lump in my throat. We both know he can't make that promise, but pointing it out isn't going to help anything.

"Kill me first," I blurt. "Before you let them take me. Kill me rather than let it happen."

"Hey, look at me," he says, tucking a finger under my chin and making me meet his eye. "No one's going to die."

My breath catches in my throat for a moment, then I jerk my head away and look at the floor. Us and lifts. We've come a long way since the first time he did that to me here.

"What's the plan?"

"Stay close to me and don't speak to anyone. If we get stopped, let me do the talking."

Gladly. My throat's so dry right now I don't think I could get any words out, anyway. Walking's going to be hard enough, my legs are shaking worse than Bambi's. So are my hands, and my stomach's churning. I think I'm going to puke.

There's a bleep and the doors slide open again, revealing the lobby. I suck in a deep breath of the stale air and force myself to move, keeping close to Scott. There's no one guarding the door – Daniel isn't going to be guarding anything again, and Joe's not coming back to his post anytime soon, either.

We just have to cross the laminated floor, and we're out of here. A handful of steps separate us from freedom.

We make it halfway there before the voice sounds from behind us.

"Hey!"

Scott presses his hand to my back and keeps us moving. Footsteps hurry behind us.

"Hey, guys."

From the corner of my eye, I see the hand reach out and grab Scott's shoulder. He tenses a split second before I register the tone of the voice. Confused, not confrontational. I turn us around, trying to force a smile onto my face. I feel Scott's hand sliding down to the pistol tucked in my waistband.

"Darren," Scott says, wearing a far more convincing smile than mine. "How's it going?"

"Didn't you hear the alarm? We're going into lockdown."

Scott's smile wavers and he starts to ease the weapon loose.

"Training accident," I blurt, before Scott can add to our body count. Darren's a friend. No one else needs to get hurt. And no one else is going to die. "He needs a hospital."

Scott pulls out his injured hand and holds it up.

"The med-floor's already sealed off. I figure we've got enough able-bodied agents that no one will miss us."

Darren winces.

"Ouch. Go on, get out of here before I lock the lobby down. I'll sign you out."

We don't wait for a second invite. We hurry out of the building and down the three stone steps. I grab the car keys from Scott's pocket – no way can he drive with that hand – and scramble behind the wheel. The second his door slams shut, I hit the gas and get us moving. I'm not going to be happy until we're a lot of miles from this place. Probably not even then.

Something digs painfully into my back as I swing us round the corner. Dammit, the gun. I left the safety on, right? Last thing I need is to be shooting myself in the

254

arse. Plenty of people want to do that for me. I reach behind me and try to pull it free. The car lurches as we hit a pothole, almost sending us ploughing into the oncoming traffic. I grab the wheel and wrench us back on course.

"Here, I've got it," Scott says. I shoot a glance at him, then lean forward. He pulls the weapon out and tosses it in the glove compartment, then leans back in his seat. I can feel his eyes on me but resist the urge to look at him again. We've had enough near misses for today.

"Anna?"

"Yeah?"

"Do you think you could slow down, maybe a little?"

I glance down at the speedo, which is a bad idea because when you're driving at nearly double the speed limit, you really need to be looking where you're going.

"Nuh-uh." We're still way too close to Langford for comfort. Gardiner might be dead, but it won't be long before someone works out what happens and comes after us. I don't plan on sticking around to find out who that might be.

"You know we've only got the one car, right?"

I ease up on the pedal a little. Not enough to bring us back inside the legal limit, but enough that we're not likely to end up wrapped around a lamppost. I don't fancy walking.

"Where exactly are we going in such a hurry?"

"A hospital, obviously."

"We can't go to a hospital."

He's looking at me like I'm crazy, which is rich. He's the one whose hand is twice the size it should be.

"You think that's going to heal up on its own?"

"I think a hospital is the first place they'll look for us."

Shit. He's right, as always. After everything, all of this, I still don't know the first thing about how to run from them. At least this time I'm not on my own. I exhale slowly and loosen my death grip on the wheel.

"So, where do we go?"

Scott is silent for a moment, then pulls a map from the glove compartment.

"I know a place we can lie low for a few days."

Chapter Twenty-One

Our times passes in a blur. We're holed up in a remote cottage nestled on the edge of the mountains. It's owned by an old friend of Scott's, who only uses it during the summer. It's small and quaint, with beautiful stone floors and exposed beams; the picture of nineteenth century charm. It's so quiet and isolated. In another lifetime, it might have been peaceful. The view over the mountains stretches for miles, and I can't stop looking out of the windows. But it's not to appreciate the picturesque scenery – I'm searching for cars and choppers disrupting it and announcing that AbGen have found us.

Scott says we can only spend a couple more nights here. Soon we'll have to get moving again. Staying in one place for too long is a bad idea. It only takes one person to come sniffing around and we'll be right back on AbGen's radar. But for the moment, it's as close to peaceful as we're going to get.

I let the curtain drop and step away from the window.

"All quiet on the western front?" Scott asks with a hint of a smile tugging at the corner of his mouth. He spends as much time watching me as I do watching the scenery.

"That's east," I say, wandering away from the window. He grabs my hand and pulls me down onto his lap, careful to keep his right hand out of the way. I snuggle into him, opening my mouth to give him another lecture about hospitals. He cuts me off with a kiss – fiendish genius – and my objections melt away. I can lecture him later. Much later. Our kiss deepens, until AbGen is just a bad memory and the outside world a rumour. Nothing else is real, only this room. Only this moment.

It can't last, though. None of it. Because the outside world *is* real, and AbGen are coming for us.

"Where are we going to go?" I ask him.

"Now? You're asking me about this now?"

He reaches down for another kiss, but I press my finger to his lips, keeping him at bay with a smile.

"Now. While you're properly motivated."

"You drive me crazy," he objects, trying again for a kiss that I deny him.

"I didn't hear you complaining about that last night."

I remove myself from his lap with a wicked grin, trailing my hand across his arms. He grunts, half frustration, half amusement, and rolls his head back to watch me.

"Come on, oh masterful tactician. Where do we go from here?"

"Did you hear that?" He twists his head right to the window.

"Yeah, nice try. Just admit you don't have all the answers."

He shakes his head and cocks an ear towards the door. I freeze. He's serious. And that's when I hear it. The low, throaty rumble of an engine.

I straighten up in a heartbeat, casting a frantic look around the room. My eyes fix on one of the guns we stole from AbGen and I snatch it up. The other's in the vehicle, but it doesn't matter because Scott can't shoot left-handed. The noise grows louder as I slide the magazine into the well and chamber a round. A car engine, and it's close.

"No messing around, Anna. The first sign of trouble, you shift out."

Like I'm going to do that. I ignore him and press my back up against the wall beside the door. Scott joins me, though I don't know what he thinks he's going to do with no weapon and his hand still out of action. Then again, he managed to take Marcus down. I frown as a thought strikes me.

"You can't sense anything?" I breathe, my voice barely a whisper. He shakes his head in response and my frown deepens. Whoever's coming, they're not an absa. Did AbGen send a team made up entirely of handlers so

Scott couldn't feel them coming? And how the hell did they find us out here?

The rumble of the engine cuts off abruptly. I strain my ears, listening for the sounds of the team surrounding us above the pounding of my heart. I can just make out the crunch of footsteps on the cottage's uneven track. But it only sounds like one pair. The rest of them must be going round the back. My fingers are itching to peel back the curtain a crack and look out into the falling darkness, but I don't dare move from this spot. The footsteps come closer. There's a scraping in the lock – a lock pick? – and the door edges inwards. It gets halfway before Scott's left hand snakes through it. He pulls back, dragging a figure inside and slamming him against the wall. Damn, he's strong. His foot kicks the door shut and I lurch forward, jamming my gun against the figure's head.

I take him in with a glance – male, athletic, no radio in his ear, weapon in his hand is… a baseball bat? It tumbles to the floor as the man's wide eyes take me in.

"Anna, stop!"

I snap my head round to Scott. He releases the intruder and steps back.

"What's going on?"

The man, wisely, says nothing, but he's not acting like any agent I've ever met. Who the hell breaches a holed-up subject with a damned baseball bat? I kick it aside anyway, because weird doesn't translate as trustworthy.

"It's Peter," Scott says. "He owns this place."

I stare from one man to the other for a long moment, breathing heavily, before I lower the gun and step back, still keeping a wary eye on our visitor while my brain catches up. The owner. I guess there was always a chance he'd get wind we were camping out down here. Probably just as well I didn't shoot him.

"Scott," Peter says stiffly, inclining his head a fraction in greeting. "Who's your friend?"

"Uh, this is Anna. We needed a place to lie low for a couple of days."

"Hi." I give him an embarrassed smile and a little wave with the hand that isn't currently wrapped around a gun. "Want some coffee?"

I put the kettle on while Peter explains that he came to check the place out after a friend had seen smoke coming from the chimney. Squatters are a bigger problem than you'd expect in this part of the country, apparently.

"So how do you two know each other?" I ask, passing a steaming mug to Scott's friend. He shoots a quick glance at Scott, who nods.

"She's clued in."

I stiffen, almost spilling my coffee, because I've got an uneasy feeling in my stomach about where this is going. There's only one secret I'm clued in on.

"I used to be a handler at AbGen." He must see the alarm on my face because he quickly adds, "I haven't been back there in years."

I guess the handler retirement package is a little better than the one they offer absas. Makes sense, I guess. They can always train more handlers. Sucks to be wanted.

"I take it you two don't work there anymore, either?" Peter says, watching us carefully over the rim of his mug. His eyes flicker to Scott's damaged hand cradled in his lap. I don't know how much we can trust him, so I leave Scott to do the talking.

"We're exploring other options," Scott says. "Maybe you can help. Have you ever heard of something called the Ishmaelians?"

Peter considers it for a moment, then shakes his head.

"Sorry, can't say I have. You might try speaking to Carson."

"Derrick Carson?"

Peter nods, then drains the rest of his coffee from his cup and sets it aside.

"I should get going. Those tracks are treacherous after dark."

He pushes himself up from the armchair and heads for the door. Once he reaches it, he turns back and looks at us both.

"You two are welcome to stay here as long as you like, but I don't want to get tangled up with AbGen again. If they start asking about you, I won't lie. But for what it's worth, I won't be the one to contact them."

"Thanks," Scott says, clasping hands with the man. "I – we – appreciate it."

"Any time." He looks over at me. "Anna, it was nice meeting you."

"And you. Sorry about, you know, the gun thing."

His lips curve up into a brief smile, and he taps a hand over his heart.

"Helps to keep the old ticker beating."

The door closes behind him, and I set my mug down with a sigh. That was too close for comfort.

"Do you trust him?"

Scott nods and sinks back into the worn sofa.

"He won't tell anyone we're here. But we shouldn't stick around for too much longer. Every day we stay puts him in more danger."

"Then," I say, curling up on the sofa next to him, "I take it we have a plan now?"

"We're heading north, first thing tomorrow," he says. "We'll track down Carson and see if he knows anything about the Ishmaelians."

Yeah, the Ishmaelians. I lean my head back. Whatever, whoever that might be. A place? An organisation? A damned rock band? Our best chance of bringing down AbGen, I know that much. And maybe our only chance of surviving Gardiner's legacy. Or the fastest way of getting ourselves killed.

"What about Joe? Maybe he managed to convince the others that–"

Scott cuts me off with a shake of his head.

"If it was safe, he'd have reached out to us by now."

"How? By sending a raven?" I gesture to the room around us. "We're a little off the grid out here. Even Peter only stumbled across us by chance."

"He'd have found a way. A TV report or an article in the newspaper."

"Oh."

I drop my head onto Scott's shoulder. We're silent for a moment until I say, in a quiet voice,

"We don't have to look for them."

Scott smooths a lock of my hair aside so he can see my face.

"We can't run forever."

"We could," I object. Because if running looks like this, the two of us holed up somewhere together, then I'd run for an eternity. I sigh. "But it's not just about us."

He nods. We've both left friends behind, friends we can't risk getting in touch with, friends who deserve to know the truth about AbGen, and never will. Not if we keep running.

"North?" I ask, and he answers me with a nod.

"First thing tomorrow."

A mischievous grin returns to my eyes, and I place my palm onto his firm chest.

"That means we've still got tonight."

I close my lips over his, and the rest of the world ceases to exist. No AbGen, no absas and handlers, no Ishmaelians. Just me and Scott. Just two people who love each other. We're safe, and we're together, and nothing else matters.

A note from the author

Thank you for sharing part one of Anna and Scott's journey with me. To find out what happens next, be sure to check out TALENTBORN:EXILED, book two in the TALENTBORN series.

Meanwhile, if you enjoyed this book, I'd be really grateful if you would take a moment to leave me a review.

Sign up to my newsletter by visiting www.cschurton.com to be kept up to date with my new releases and received exclusive content.

There's one thing I love almost as much as writing, and that's hearing from people who have read and enjoyed my books. If you've got a question or a comment about the series, you can connect with me and other like-minded people over in my readers' group at www.facebook.com/groups/CSChurtonReaders

Printed in Great Britain
by Amazon